The Mighty Currawongs

⊰ THE ⊱

Mighty Currawongs

& other stories

BRIAN DOYLE

Red Hen Press | *Pasadena, CA*

Book layout by Mark E. Cull

Library of Congress Cataloging-in-Publication Data

Names: Doyle, Brian, 1956 November 6– author.
Title: The mighty Currawongs : & other stories / Brian Doyle.
Description: First edition. | Pasadena, CA : Red Hen Press, [2016]
Identifiers: LCCN 2016023192 (print) | LCCN 2016029629
    (ebook) | ISBN 9781597090520 (softcover : acid-free paper) | ISBN
    9781597095082
Subjects: | BISAC: FICTION / Short Stories (single author).
Classification: LCC PS3604.O9547 A6 2016 (print) | LCC PS3604.
    O9547 (ebook) | DDC 813/.6—dc23
LC record available at https://lccn.loc.gov/2016023192

The National Endowment for the Arts, the Los Angeles County Arts Commission, the Los Angeles Department of Cultural Affairs, the Dwight Stuart Youth Fund, the Pasadena Arts & Culture Commission and the City of Pasadena Cultural Affairs Division, Sony Pictures Entertainment, and the Ahmanson Foundation partially support Red Hen Press.

First Edition
Published by Red Hen Press
www.redhen.org

Provenance & Birth Records

"The Mighty Currawongs" appeared in the fine Australian e-zine *Eureka Street*, thanks to the discerning and entertaining editor Tim Kroenert, a Collingwood Magpies fan, the poor lad.

"Guys Who Knew Guys" and "The People of West Kalimantan vs. the Glorious Kayan Warriors of Borneo" appeared in the wild Oregon e-zine *Smokebox*, thanks to editors John Richen and Marc Covert, and if you have never read *Smokebox* go to smokebox.net and paw through their great archive of the inimitable David James Duncan, who is a visionary nut.

"Elson Habib, Playing White, Ponders His Opening Move" and "Mr Oleander" appeared in *The Sun*, thanks to editors Sy Safransky, Andrew Snee, and Tim McKee. Lovely magazine, *The Sun*, and supported wholly by its subscribers, no advertisements, a rare bird. Cool magazine, with nuggets of great in every issue.

"The Mermens" appeared in *Inscape*, the student-edited literary magazine at Brigham Young University in Utah; my particular thanks to the fine essayist Patrick Madden there for foisting this odd adventure on the students, who, to their credit, laughed; laughter being a sign of religious and spiritual maturity, seems to me.

"The New Bishop" appeared in *TriQuarterly Online*, an electric magazine from Northwestern University in Illinois. My thanks to Managing Editor Amanda Morris.

"A Note on the Actors" and "On Flinging the Dog" both appeared in *Lurch*, an e-zine published, irregularly but entertainingly, in Brooklyn, New York, USA.

"Dear Mum" appeared in *Platform Magazine* in Melbourne, Australia, published by Victoria University and edited by the energetic smiling Bruno Lettieri. Hi Bruno!

"The Subtle Theater" and "The Seventh" appeared in *U.S. Catholic* magazine, published in Chicago by the Claretian Missionaries, an admirable order of priests and brothers. My particular thanks to editor Cathy O'Connell-Cahill.

"Roma vs. Lazio," "The Detours," "The Guest Speaker," and "Elson Habib, Playing Black, Ponders the End Game" appeared in *New Letters*, from the U. of Missouri at Kansas City, courtesy of the estimable

Robert Stewart. Fact: Bob Stewart is one of the great editors in America and has been so for a long time. Great editors are subtle and valuable creatures and someone should say so once in a while.

"Four Boston Basketball Stories" and "Chauncy Street" appeared in *The Kenyon Review*, and when I have dark days I cheer myself up thinking that Flannery O'Connor was published there, and so was I, so we are cousins now, sort of, a little.

"Muirin" appeared in *Saint Anthony Messenger* magazine, published by the Franciscans, a very fine Catholic order of priests and nuns and brothers, I have to say. Their founder was a genius.

"A Surf Story" appeared in *Kauai Backstory*, courtesy of Kim Rogers.

"The Lutheran Minister's Daughter" I dedicate, with high glee, to my friend Father Tom Doyle, of the Congregation of Holy Cross at the University of Notre Dame, who, I kid you not, before he became a terrific priest, fell in love with the Lutheran minister's daughter in his town, and I think it was the very phrase *I fell in love with the Lutheran minister's daughter* that set me to eventually dreaming this story. Thank you, Thomas.

For Cynthia Ozick,
with gratitude and admiration

Contents

1 ~ A Surf Story

3 ~ This Is the Part
  Where You Say Something Real

6 ~ The Archbishop Loses His Faith

16 ~ Four Boston Basketball Stories

24 ~ In the Café Rue de Turenne,
  Charleroi, Belgium, 1943

27 ~ Mr Kim's Song

31 ~ Roma vs. Lazio

36 ~ Dear Mum,

39 ~ Mr Oleander

43 ~ The Mighty Currawongs

47 ~ Jesus Joseph

56 ~ The Detours

62 ~ Chauncy Street

66 ~ Guys Who Knew Guys

68 ~ Elson Habib, Playing White,
  Ponders His Opening Move

72 ~ Elson Habib, Playing Black,
  Ponders the End Game

77 ~ Her Kid

80 ~ The Mermens

82 ~ The Stigmata

86 ~ The People of West Kalimantan vs.
       the Glorious Kayan Warriors of Borneo

89 ~ The Lutheran Minister's Daughter

92 ~ The New Bishop

97 ~ A Note on the Actors

100 ~ The Subtle Theater

108 ~ On Flinging the Dog

110 ~ A Note on Countification

115 ~ KXMS

121 ~ When You're Out of Schlitz,
        You're Out of Beer

124 ~ It's All About Teeth, in the End

126 ~ The Guest Speaker

131 ~ Sachiel the Tailor

133 ~Muirin

136 ~ The Seventh

The Mighty Currawongs

A Surf Story

I'll tell you a surfing story, and this is the rare surf story that has no oceans or surfboards in it, because it's about a guy who spent almost his whole life surfing situations and relationships, never falling in, never over his head, never breathless, always on top of the situation and never of it, you know what I mean? And he got almost to the end of his life without ever getting his feet wet, and then, as so often is the case when we talk about hearts being startled awake, it was a kid who knocked him off his board and into the sea where hearts get hammered and startled and shivered and whole.

But I get ahead of myself. The guy's name was Pete. He had been a terrific athlete as a kid and then he was a terrific hand with money and investments. He made boatloads of money, got lots of girls, traveled everywhere, did every dashing thing you can imagine, but after a while even the coolest girls would gently disentangle themselves, because, as one of them said with real affection, you never get tangled, Pete, and in the end we see that you don't want to bother, and even someone who just wants to have fun can't stay long, you know what I mean?

He did know what she meant, too, which is what stung.

He got all the way to age fifty like this, looking cool on the outside and not getting birthday cards from anyone, and no one except the doorman at his condo knowing when he was sick with the flu, and finally he sold his condo in Boston and bagged his lucrative master of the universe job and moved to Poipu and bought a condo on the beach and spent his time paddle-surfing, but nothing really changed and he had girls but no lovers and companions but no friends, you know what I mean? But finally what happened was he was driving drunk and got busted, and during the whole process of getting that fixed he met a detective who showed him the world of meth babies, kids whose parents were addicts and dumped them or burned them with cigarettes and dangled them from highway overpasses and evil shit like that, and there was a kid named Kimmo who was four and both parents dead in meth explosions, and this kid says to Pete one day, at the cop orphanage, how come you never look at me with both your eyes? and Pete says that was the moment everything cracked. He says it wasn't like in the movies where there's swelling music and the lights get brighter, in fact he said he wanted to slap the kid for being rude, but he didn't, and eventually he adopted Kimmo, it's a long story and there's no happy ending neither, because they argue like hell, and neither one of them can cook worth two cents as yet, and Kimmo just got his face tattooed like a Maori for some reason, which sent Pete into a fit like you read about.

But he's not surfing anymore is the point, you know what I mean?

This Is the Part
Where You Say Something Real

I'd love to begin with some comedy about regulations for having roaring scorching arguments in cars, so we could all start out laughing, rules like *no fussing with the radio during an argument*, and *keep both hands where your debating partner can see them*, and *no bringing up past boyfriends*, and things like that, but the fact is that arguing in cars isn't funny, and a lot of hearts are broken in cars, the party of the first part fiddling with the mirrors and banging his fist against the steering wheel and staring out the driver's window in exasperation and despair, and the party of the second part staring out her window and fidgeting with her scarf and searching the glove compartment for tissues with which to dry the tears occasioned by the party of the first part, tissues she could have sworn she put there for just such emergencies, but which were, he says quietly, borrowed by one of their children for a school project in which *someone* was supposed to have procured artificial snow, but someone totally spaced out, and someone then of course blamed *dad* for not being prescient enough to know that artificial snow was required for the project, which dad did not know there even *was* such a project, and had to improvise.

This makes her laugh through her tears and then there's a throb of silence.

Nor did I know, says the party of the first part, that there actually is such a thing as artificial snow, did you know there are all kinds of artificial snow, and you can buy it in bags of various sizes, not to mention spray cans of every size imaginable, and there are even snow blowers designed specifically for artificial snow, who knew?

This is why I think we should get divorced, she says. You care about stuff like that and I don't, and I care about stuff like mold in the basement and you say you do but you don't, and after twenty years the fact is that we are never going to care about what the other one cares about. The only thing we care about together is the kids.

You want me to care more about mold? he says. I care plenty about mold. There are like a hundred kinds of mold, and they mostly have names like monsters: Stachybotrys and Aspergillus and Cladosporium, that kind of thing. I think what we have is Stachybotrys. I checked photographs.

You have to have some kind of shared dream to be able to go on, she says.

He notices that his breath on the window makes a perfect circle of condensation, exactly two inches in diameter north to south and east to west. He refrains from pointing this out to the party of the second part.

This is the part where you say something real, she says.

I hate arguing in cars, he says. I been arguing in cars since I was nineteen years old. I have also argued in buses and trains. Not on planes though. You wonder why. I mean, a plane is just as public a place as a bus or a train or a street. Argued in plenty of streets. Also lanes, alleys, drives, circles, boulevards, roads, and highways. Remember the argument we had in that convertible on the highway in the desert where that truck almost mashed us like a skunk? You made a terrific save there. Save of the century. Reflexes like a cat.

I remember that, she says.

And remember the argument we had that time in the city plaza when a cop gave us a ticket for disturbing the peace, remember that?

Yes, she says.

And the argument we had every time we were going to name a kid?

That's because you wanted to name them for vegetables and symphonies.

And fish. Trout, wouldn't that be a cool name? Trout McPhee. Sounds like a novelist, or the guy in charge of Dartmouth College endowed funds.

I don't know if I can do this anymore, she says.

They sit silent for a moment with ten thousand thoughts and emotions and memories and stories and jokes and anecdotes and complaints and revelations seething.

Look, he says, I don't have anything wise or cool or romantic to say. I don't know anything about anything. I just like you and our kids more than anything else in the world. That's all I got for you. I got no promises of any kind whatsoever for anyone. I have no idea what's going to happen. I swear I'll do my best for you and for them but I could have an affair tomorrow and so could you and they could get hit by a car tomorrow or get cancer and that's that. All I got is who I am. If you want to get divorced we'll get divorced. I like you, is all. I don't have convictions about marriage and family anymore. I don't have convictions about anything whatsoever. I just go along trying to be honest and kind and pay attention to who you are and who they are. That's all I got for you.

They sit silent a while.

We better go in, she says. I see them staring out the upstairs window.

You need a tissue?

I need major artificial snow, she says. I need new sneakers for two teenage children even though I bought new sneakers for them three weeks ago. I need a week at the beach alone. I need serious retirement funds. I need a new basement. I need some electricity in my love life. I need to know that the man I love knows me in my deepest inner heart even though that's scary for him and for me. I need more from you than to be my dear friend but I don't know how to get there or if you can or if I can. I need a lot of things I am never going to get and most of the time I am cool with that but sometimes I can't bear it anymore. Sometimes I just cannot bear it one more minute. Did you remember to buy toilet paper and coffee beans?

The Archbishop Loses His Faith

It was during the Christmas gathering for Catholic finance professionals at the country club that the archbishop lost his faith, right after the salad course, and just before he was supposed to offer brief and cheerful remarks to the gathering. The salad was excellent—it wasn't the *salad's* fault, that's for sure—but just as the waitress came for his plate he felt his faith leave him as quickly and thoroughly as water through a collapsed dam. One minute it was there, and the next it was gone, as if it had suddenly drained away through a widening crack.

He sat silently, rattled.

The situation was even worse because he was now expected to rise and offer brief and cheerful remarks. This was pro forma, he knew—no one wanted to hear a sermon or a speech at this juncture—but still, he was supposed to stand, and while appearing dignifiedly episcopal, say something wry, thank the audience for having him as a guest, thank them for their work for the church, and then finish with a joke or a blessing, whichever seemed best. He knew the drill; how many thousands of times in his career had he been in exactly this situation, and handled it with his usual easy aplomb? Many thousands.

Not this time, though. He stared at the tablecloth for a moment. The finance professionals, many of them high officers of their companies, waited respectfully as the archbishop seemed to be gathering his thoughts. The waiters and waitresses seized the momentary pause in the burble to offer more wine—chardonnay or cabernet, Your Excellency?

Neither right now, thank you, Megan.

Certainly the archbishop had lost his faith before—many times, if he was being honest and forthright about it. But always before, it had been a brief interlude, and he had been able to call on the Madonna for help, and soon enough he would feel a sort of warm blue peace flow back into him like a transfusion; often, curiously, after someone touched his hand, or he heard someone sing. But this—this was different. He felt . . . bereft. He felt like a jacket without a person inside it, to be honest. But circumstances dictated that he rise, and smile, and in his usual crisp amused voice say something brief and cheerful, and then close with a small joke, which he did, using one of his standards: gently chiding Martin Luther for ruining a perfectly good door when he hammered his Theses to the church in Wittenberg.

Our brother Martin was absolutely right to excoriate the sale of indulgences, said the archbishop with a smile, but could he not have used duct tape, or chewing gum?

This got the usual chuckle, even though many of the men and women in the room had heard the joke before, and the archbishop sat down, now utterly rattled; he had been ready to finish with a blessing, but he could not form the words; it was as if his mouth was empty of anything except a jape, and well-worn one, at that.

The waitress again offered him wine with the entrée—it's roast beef, Your Excellency, and the cabernet is very good—but he again declined politely.

His neighbor to his left was the chief financial officer of a large health care concern and a good friend, but as he leaned in to make conversation about Notre Dame football, the archbishop had trouble focusing on his words. Just as it was time for him to make some sort of reply, even a placeholder like *really?* or *is that so?*, his neighbor to his right leaned in and asked him about his plans over the holidays. Any travel, Archbishop? The Holy Land? The Notre Dame game?

No, no, said the archbishop. The press of duty, and then perhaps a few days at the coast. I find travel during the holidays exhausting, to be honest. And I am not getting younger, that's for sure.

Oh, you will outlive us all, said the man to his right, a fund manager. You have stacked up fifty years of extra credit, Your Excellency, and surely God will grant you an extra couple of decades. You'll outlive Archbishop Halloran, and he lived to be 104, as you remember.

Ascribing all the credit for longevity to eating fish and smoking cigars, said the neighbor to his left, and they laughed, and the archbishop excused himself.

In the men's room he gripped the marble counter so hard that his knuckles went pale. In the mirror he could see that his face, usually avuncular despite its narrowness, was haggard, and he seemed two shades whiter than he had been when he arrived at the country club. Oh, Mary, please, he thought. Please? I feel empty and alone and silly in this uniform and this event and this body without your light and love giving me strength. I am weary and old and you have ever been my compass. Please?

But no transfusion came, and his soul shriveled even more.

Just then the door sighed open and another man came in to wash his hands. This was the federal circuit court judge in the city, technically not a finance professional, but invited to the Christmas gathering every year on general principle. A brilliant man, the archbishop had always thought; very conservative indeed, but not adamant or brittle about it, and not one to lecture anyone else publicly or privately about their conduct or convictions. The archbishop had always rather liked the judge, though they had spent little time together; part of the reason he liked the man, he thought now, was that the judge was confident but quiet, and so many men around the archbishop were neither of those things.

Are you not well, sir? asked the judge. You seem a little... unmoored.

The advent of a cold, I suspect, said the archbishop. Thanks, though.

Sir, he thought—deft touch. *Your Excellency* is florid, *Archbishop* is a cold title, and no one has called me *Father* for thirty years now. Let alone John or Johnny.

Just thinking the word *Johnny* made him think of his childhood in Chicago, and kids yelling his name in the street, and his mother's floury hands, and his sisters laughing and weeping at his ordination on the lakefront. Our Johnny! they had wept. Our little Johnny! It had been a wild wet day, and he remembered the way his sisters all stood together by the seawall, their dresses and scarves whipping and lashing in the wind.

Can I be of assistance at all, sir? said the judge gently, and the archbishop stared at him for an instant and then said, to his own surprise, Yes, Diarmuid. Yes, I hope you can. I have lost my faith. I have mislaid or misplaced it, perhaps. Has this happened to you?

Yes, sir, said the judge. Almost every day. Every other day for fifty years. I lost it when I was thirteen years old and I have to regain it almost every day. Occasionally a few days will pass when I thirst and there is naught for me to drink. During those days I am a man lost in a great wilderness and there is no one to lead me in the darkness.

What do you do?

Pray. Fast. Walk along the river or the ocean. Water seems to help. When I am fully and truly desperate I appeal to Maureen for counsel and comfort. My wife.

But of wives I have none, said the archbishop, and some part of his brain heard himself say the phrase, and wonder giddily, am I in a Shakespeare play or what?

We should step outside, sir, said the judge, extending a hand, and he and the archbishop walked into the paneled hallway arm in arm like old and boon companions. Just as they emerged, however, two of the finance professionals approached eagerly, and the judge, smoothly turning the archbishop toward the bar, made some sort of subtle gesture with his hand to the financiers, who understood the signal as a call for privacy in a matter of great import, and retreated.

The judge led the archbishop through the empty bar, through what seemed to be a very well-appointed locker room, and finally to a small narrow dim kitchen that smelled powerfully and alluringly of cinnamon and nutmeg; if ever there was a room that smelled like pie, thought the archbishop, this is the one.

Is this where pies are made? he asked.

Perhaps so, said the judge. This is where the staff makes breakfast for anyone here early in the morning. There's a much larger official kitchen, where the renowned chefs ply their trade, but this one is something of a secret. I believe it was a cloakroom in the old days. The building was a house before it was a clubhouse, you know.

I thirst and there is naught for me to drink, said the archbishop, almost whispering.

Have you . . . talked to His Mother?

I have. She has always been there before. She is silent now.

They sat silently for a moment.

Can you go on? asked the judge, gently.

I don't see how, said the archbishop. Not to be dramatic. I mean, I can play the part, I am very good at that, but the whole essence of the thing is that you have hope, you have a feeling in every part of your body and mind. It has nothing to do with sense and logic and reason and everything to do with trust. Perhaps like marriage. If you did not *believe* in her, then you would not be truly married, is that right?

Something like that, said the judge, although I have only been married once, and am not as experienced as other men. And you can be married without faith and trust, although I would call that more of a business proposition than a sacrament.

I admire a nutritious marriage, said the archbishop. I do. People tease priests for not knowing anything about marriage but of course we do. What you yearn for, you study deeply and thoroughly, trust me.

I do trust you, said the judge quietly.

Thank you.

Also I find that children refresh me when I am dessicated, said the judge. But then I have grandchildren here, and thus easy access to joy.

Of children and their children I have none, nor prospects thereof, said the archbishop, and this time he grinned at the orotundity of the phrase, as did the judge.

But then the emptiness arose in the archbishop again and he must have winced, for the judge put his hand on the archbishop's shoulder, just as you would with a son who had just opened a Dear John letter from his girlfriend.

It has nothing to do with religion, said the archbishop, so quietly that the judge had to lean in a little closer to catch his murmur. It's about mercy and some kind of coherence. I don't ask that the world make sense. It *doesn't* make sense. It just is. It's the strangest and most painful of miracles. It is itself. It has nothing to do with religion at all. And I love and esteem our religion. I have the utmost respect for almost all religions. But you have to have some kind of belief that there's peace and mercy and laughter available. That we are here for each other somehow. That the things we design to carry that impulse make a sort of shabby sense in the long term—religions, families, clans, teams, countries. It's not *about* religion. It's about . . . conviction. You can't *think* your way to it. That's why theology is so funny in the end, arguing about who's right and wrong about things that are light years beyond right and wrong. I say this with all respect to the Church Eternal. But we all know we are not the only way. There are many ways. But I have lost my way.

You've lost it before but you always find it again, isn't that so? said the judge.

Yes.

Perhaps patience?

Yes.

The judge was exquisitely aware that this suggestion was not particularly helpful, but he was wise enough not to pile more suggestions into the breach; that was a common sin, he thought, the urge to tell others what to do in situations where no advice was needed, wanted, or useful. And quite clearly this was one of those situations.

The first time this happened was on my ordination day, isn't that funny? said the archbishop. About an hour after the ceremony. We were driving home from the lakefront, and I lost my faith somewhere near Cicero Avenue. Very deflating. I didn't tell anyone. My sisters noticed but they didn't say anything. It flooded back into me that evening. Children playing in the street. The rain had finally stopped and children came flying out of their apartment buildings like swifts leaving their nests at dusk. What a cacophony! And something came flooding back into me just at that moment, as if I was a vessel being filled again after being dry. A very rattling and thrilling experience. To some degree I was relieved and delighted to have faced that frontier and come through it; I was that rare boy who never doubted, even as a teenager, even as a young man, during the very years when you must doubt everything you were ever taught, so as to find what it is you believe.

I know the feeling, said the judge. All too well. My first time was when I was thirteen and playing football. I had just been handed the ball for a sweep and I suddenly thought everything I'd ever been told by my parents and pastor might well be utter nonsense. This thought had never occurred to me before. A *shattering* thought, that's the right word.

What happened to the football play, the sweep? asked the archbishop, with a smile.

Oh, I got hammered, said the judge. I think four defenders hit me at once. I had slowed down and allowed space between me and my blockers and I paid dearly. My chest is still sore on the coldest days.

People say this is depression, said the archbishop, that those of us who lose our faith are bipolar, but that's not it either. It's not about religion. It's about faith. It's like your gas tank is emptied in a split second, and you cannot see any possible way you will ever get a drop of fuel ever again. I keep coming back to the word dessicated. A cracked crumbling shrieking desert where a moment before there had been a wide and shining lake.

Just then the same two finance professionals who had approached the archbishop in the hallway approached again, genuinely concerned for his welfare. One had his arms open as if to embrace the archbishop and the other had his hands folded as if in nervous prayer.

Your Excellency . . . ?

Just a little indisposed, Martin, said the archbishop. Thanks for your concern, and you too, Michael. How kind of you to think of me.

Could I call your driver, Your Excellency?

No, no, Martin, said the archbishop. I'll be fine. Just a moment to rest, I think. If you and Michael would be so good as to make my apologies to the rest of the men I would be most grateful. I think I'll just head home at this point. You understand. Good thing there are no boring after-dinner remarks expected of me.

You couldn't be boring if you tried, Your Excellency, said Michael.

Now, Michael, said the archbishop, you do not want to issue such bold lies to your archbishop. Gentlemen, my thanks and prayers for your families.

The two men understood the signal and withdrew, and the archbishop stood to leave. The judge stood also, feeling as if he ought to stay with the archbishop but not knowing quite how to engineer it. For a moment they stood, looking at each other, and then the archbishop said, again very quietly, I am most grateful for the kindness in your soul, Diarmuid. Most grateful. How we will go on I do not know, but I am very happy to have a companion, as it were.

You and me both, sir, said the judge. If you don't mind perhaps I can stop by the chancery this week and see how we are doing on the journey.

I'd like that, said the archbishop. Come by anytime.

I'll call Rosemary about your schedule, said the judge.

No, said the archbishop. No. Just come by. The door's open.

Just then the waitress came in with a plate of roast beef in one hand and a glass of red wine in the other. Oh, sir, she said to the archbishop, you must forgive me for not noticing you were gone so long, but I saved a plate for you, and this is the best red wine we have, says the steward. It's not the cabernet. I think it's nebbiolo, or dolcetto. He said *you* would know at the first sip. He said that cabernet is for people who want red wine and this wine is for people who want good wine. He says you know more about good wine than he does even though you hardly ever have a glass. He says if you ever want to give up your day job you can come work for him, or he will work for you, whichever you prefer. He says you can even keep your black uniform if you want, or you can go white or maroon or whatever.

The judge smiled at her headlong good humor, as did the arch-bishop, who accepted the plate and glass but then laid them gently on the counter behind him and turned back to the waitress.

Megan, this is such a kindness, to think of me, he said, but I am afraid I had better not eat or drink for a bit. A slight indisposition. But how generous of you and Thomas to think of me. You have lifted my heart and I am most grateful. And do thank Thomas for me, and tell him I will consider his offer of employment very carefully. Retirement age approacheth and I could use a real job after these many years in the theater, as it were.

She smiled and then took a half-step back without effort, as dancers do, and suddenly curtsied deeply, again with a deft effortless grace, as if she were made of water, or rubber. *That* one is an athlete, or a dancer, thought the judge.

Archbishop, she said when she had risen again, may I ask you a favor? It's a little thing but a big thing to me. My grandmother gave me a rosary just before she died, and she told me to ask you to bless it for me, for her too, and she said your blessing would protect me, as long as I carried this rosary, and she would feel the instant you blessed it, she would feel it like an electric shock wherever she is, and I *loved* my gramma, sir, I loved her so much I can't stand her being gone, I can't *stand* it. I have the rosary right here, sir, and could I ask you to bless it? Please? I know you are busy and I know you are not feeling well but I'll never get the chance again, I *know* I won't, so could you bless this for me? Please?

Oh, Megan, certainly, said the archbishop, and she held up the rosary, cupped in her hands like a bird in a nest; a battered wooden rosary, the beads so old and worn that they shone darkly like coffee beans. The archbishop reached out both of his hands, long narrow hands with age spots and scars on almost all his knuckles, and held them like a tent over the rosary, and whispered a blessing. As he finished he cupped her hands in his, and closed his eyes and bowed his head, to ask for grace and peace on this kind-hearted girl and her beloved grandmother; but just as his hands touched hers he felt a shock in every atom of his body, just as if he had stuck his hand in an electric socket. For an instant he was frightened, and wondered if this was the stroke he had always secretly thought would be his fate; and then he realized what had happened, and bowed lower, and whispered *thank you*, and opened his eyes.

Both Megan and the judge were staring at him. Megan had tears in her eyes, perhaps for her grandmother, but the judge knew, and was smiling.

We should go, sir, said the judge.

We should, Diarmuid, said the archbishop. Do come by the chancery this week.

With genuine pleasure, sir, with genuine pleasure, said the judge, and they all parted, Megan back to work, the archbishop to his car near the putting green, and the judge back to the dining room, where he was welcomed back with open arms and many questions about what was on his docket and what he thought of the elections.

Four Boston Basketball Stories

Chirping & Warbling

I have written here and there about the time when I played in a
basketball league in Boston that was so tough that sometimes
guys driving to the hole lost fingers, and one time a guy driving
hard to the basket got hit so hard his right *arm* came off, but he
was lefty and hit both free throws, but there are about one million
other stories from that league, most of them true, like the guy who
showed up at one game in a Bentley and then was a guest of the
state of Massachusetts until the second round of the playoffs, and
the guys who came to games riding on a huge garbage truck their
point guard drove for work, and the guys whose girlfriends would
deliberately take their sweaters off and stretch in an ostentatious
manner at key moments of the game, and things like that, but one
story I have never told you is the time not one but both referees
were escorted from the court at halftime by plainclothes policemen,
which was not something any of us had seen before, and which re-
mains memorable, partly because the policemen were so obviously
policemen beneath their shining suits.

Their suits actually *glinted* in the brilliant lights, and we started
laughing and saying things like *are those suits made from linoleum,
man?* and *is that suit made from melted toys or what, Officer?* and
one policeman got really annoyed and stalked over to our bench
all huffy and bristly, but that just made us start laughing harder

because not only was his suit some kind of gleaming teal plastic fabric from Mars but his shoes actually, I kid you not, chirped and warbled whenever he took a step, which sent us into hysterics.

This was not going to end well at all, but the other cop, seeing his partner about to pop a gasket, hustled over to cool things down, but that was a mistake, because as soon as his attention was diverted from his prisoners they melted into the darkness beyond the sidelines. Our point guard, an alert and attentive guy, waited a while—we liked those refs, because they actually called fouls sometimes, and one of them had once called traveling on a guy on another team who used to pretty much take the bus when he drove to the basket—and then pointed this out to the second cop, while the first cop was demanding our identification cards and we were pretending to reach into our jockstraps for them. The second cop, realizing that the moment was lost, pulled his partner away, and they stalked back to their car, the first cop's shoes singing like a bird. Now, I have heard new shoes squeak and creak, we all have, but I have to say I have never before or since heard shoes chirp and warble like that. Those were really amazing shoes.

Well, we thought we were up a creek for the second half, because this was not a league you could play games in without referees, it was a tough enough league with the refs calling fouls only when there was blood or an inarguable splinter of bone on the court, but just as we were about to call it a night the two referees slid back into the light, grinning, and one guy blew his whistle to start the second half.

If I was an honest man I would have to admit that the refs gave us the benefit of the doubt on close calls the rest of the way, but we would have won that game anyway, as the other team only had five guys and one of them was just back from getting a new spleen or eye or something, and anyway both teams were not as intense about the game as usual. Several times during a break in play a guy on one team or the other would chirp or warble and we would all lose it laughing for a moment before the game resumed.

Dangling & Cursing

And yet *another* story from the men's basketball league in Boston where my friends and I played for years was the time a guy on the other team *got stuck to the basket,* which is not a sentence I have ever written before, and I have been writing sentences for fifty years, since I was five years old and writing sentences like *my sister can smoke two cigarettes at the same time when mom and dad are out of the house,* and *my sister calls me words I never heard before and neither did dad he says,* and *my sister can beat me up with one hand,* and other sentences like that, although my sister is now, no kidding, a nun in a monastery.

The guy was on the other team, this was the team which once arrived to a game all riding the point guard's garbage truck, he drove the truck in the mornings and wasn't supposed to use it other than on his garbage run, but his car died and the other guys had lost their licenses or something, and they roared up to the park in this huge clanking truck, I thought we were going to pee laughing, but they beat us that game, by eight points, because they were so peeved that we were laughing at their *mode of transport,* as our point guard said.

Anyway the second time we played them their rabbit small forward, a guy who could jump to the moon but not do anything particularly effective with the ball when he got there, drove the baseline and elevated for what he thought was going to be a shocking monster dunk which would be all the more shocking because he was skinny as a stick and you do not expect a guy who looks like he weighs about eighty pounds to be cramming the ball in traffic, but our center, who disliked anyone dunking in his lane, went up to block the shot, and a couple other of our guys went up with our center to keep him company, and the rabbit guy got twisted around somehow and lost the ball and got his wrist stuck in the steel net, so when everyone else came back down he stayed up there, dangling and cursing like a minister.

Our point guard, a terrific rebounder for his position, had slipped in and grabbed the rebound and was off to the races, and

I had gone with him, thinking there might be free money in this for me, but just as we sailed past midcourt the whistle blew and the refs called the play dead because (a) there was a guy hanging from the other basket, (b) our center and the two guys who had gone up with him to contest the rabbit were bent over laughing so hard I thought they were going to barf, (c) the guys on the other team, the refs, and the few spectators were laughing so hard I thought they were going to barf, and finally (d) the rabbit guy was cursing so angrily and kicking so furiously at our guys laughing at him that we thought his head was going to fly off.

Eventually they got him down, someone found a ladder in a parks and recreation shed, and our point guard got a technical foul for pointing out that he would have had a free basket but *someone* blew a whistle for what *someone* knew was not actually a violation of the rules, *nowhere* in the rule book did it say it was against the law for a guy to get stuck in the basket and dangle there cursing and kicking, and there was no reason for *someone* to get all flustered and rattled and stop play, but the other ref called a technical on the guy who got stuck for "abuse of equipment," which is also a phrase I have never written before, so everything evened out, and eventually we won by ten. We never did play those guys again, but to my mind we won the series by two points. It's interesting to think that the series would be exactly tied if the rabbit guy *had* dunked, but the fact of the matter is that he did not.

Stalking & Muttering

I thought I was finished telling stories about my Boston basketball league that was so stuffed with funny stories that it was like the stands were packed with stories waiting to be told, but I realize I never explained the actual roster of my team, so let's start with our power forward, the guy with a chest big enough to land an airplane on, the same guy who once started a fistfight with the other team's power forward *before the game began*, a remarkable phrase, well, this guy would, once or twice a game, rip down a rebound, often with one huge hand, and rather than toss the ball to our terrific point guard, or to the shooting guard who had played college ball and was the only truly ambidextrous player I ever saw, or to the wholly undisciplined and unpredictable small forward, he would take off like a loose truck down the court by himself, dribbling behind his back whether there were defenders near him or not, and he would roar toward the basket at full speed like a bearded aircraft carrier, and egregiously miss the layup, which every one of us knew was going to happen, which is why three of us trailed after him like hungry hounds, knowing there were free points if we hustled.

Our center, however, a tall talented con man named Stick, would never run with us on this play, for murky reasons; he claimed he just liked watching it unfold again and again, exactly the same way every time, as a rare case of something stable and trustworthy in a sea of tumult and confusion, but we thought he was just taking a breather to rest his shooting arm, which got so much use it would be smoking by the end of the game, and he would stick it in a bucket of ice, which is why everyone called him Stick.

Our shooting guard, the guy who had played college ball and could shoot and pass with either hand, was even better at ultimate frisbee and had been on a team that won the world championship in Sweden, partly because to freak out the other team he had led his team onto the field naked as jaybirds except for face paint and Mardi Gras beads, and ever after he wore a skein of bright Mardi Gras beads, even when he played basketball, which was a remarkable sight to see, a guy about six foot three wearing green Mardi Gras beads while hitting a lefty hook shot from the top of the key, which he actually did once, to win a playoff game, after which he sprinted around the court laughing, his beads flapping and skittering, a sweet sight.

Our point guard, a guy who never made a single mistake that I can remember, was the kind of guy who would cruise until something annoyed him, at which point he would morph into a grim genius, but we all *knew* this, and if he was stuck in cruise control and we needed the high-octane version we would deliberately annoy him somehow, usually with a stupid turnover, and his grim face would drop down like a mask, and he would go smoothly bonkers for a while. It got so that during his bonker runs we would all just attack the boards to get him the ball and then just sit back and watch him at work. He wasn't a big guy, so other teams underestimated him until one of these blistering runs, after which they would call time-out and stalk to the sidelines muttering the greatest compliment you can get in basketball: *who's got that guy?*

We had other guys on that team, like our backup point guard who ran into the woods to pee once at halftime and didn't come back for three games, and our backup small forward, who was about seven inches taller than me but wholly uninterested in rebounding, for religious reasons, he said, and our backup power forward, who was *very* interested in rebounding but couldn't score if you locked him in a gym alone for a week, and some other guys, but there's no more room for them here at the bottom of the page.

Soaring & Sailing

I'll tell you one more story about my basketball league in Boston, the league where one time our referees were escorted from the court at halftime by two plainclothes policemen in shiny suits, and another time a brawl broke out before the game because our power forward, a guy with a chest big enough to land an airplane on, took exception to a remark from the other team's power forward as we were warming up, and decked him, and there was a ruckus, and both teams were hit with ten technical fouls each before the game even began, so that a parade of guys went to the foul line at each end *before the opening whistle*, which is yet another sentence I have never written before. Our point guard, a bright guy, objected to the refs that it was not metaphysically possible to score points before the game officially started, for which argument he earned a technical foul, the refs being all pissy for some reason, but the other team's guy missed that shot.

Anyway this last story I wanted to tell you is about the court itself. Our summer league that year was played in a lovely little park filled with pine trees on the west side of the city, and for some reason the city, usually content to let its basketball and tennis courts molder for centuries, had actually refinished and repainted the court for the first time since the Pilgrims played on it in the seventeenth century, and there were glorious new powerful night lights that we heard were from construction of a new prison in which the contractor was caught doubling every order, and there were gleaming new steel nets, which were steel because even the city conceded that hanging nylon nets was essentially begging for theft.

This court was on a gentle little rise in the park, and was brilliantly lit in such a way that the darkness began exactly three feet past the sidelines and baselines, so that you could see a guy standing out of bounds to throw the ball in, but you couldn't see spectators, few as they were, nor could you see your teammates sprawled on the huge logs that served as benches for players. Guys subbing in for other guys during breaks in play would pop out of the darkness as suddenly as if they were coming from the dark wing of a stage, and guys subbing out would step off the court and vanish as thoroughly as if they had never been born. It was the most amazing thing. I remember many times when the ball would be flying out of bounds and a guy, usually our power forward, who loved diving for loose balls for some reason, I think because he was a big guy and liked to be briefly aloft and weightless, would soar after it like a huge bearded heron, if there was a heron with a chest big enough to land a plane on, and for an instant you would see his huge sneakers hanging in the air, about waist-high, although this was not a sight you wanted to linger over, because he was terrific at whipping the ball back over his shoulder at the speed of light, and if you stood there gaping at the odd sight of huge sneakers floating in the air against the velvet dark you would be treated to a basketball in the face at about a hundred miles an hour.

That's all I wanted to tell you, really; how the court that summer was so invitingly and lushly green, and the white lines were so brilliantly and densely white, and the steel nets shone like silver chains, and guys popped out of the dark like lanky grinning magic tricks, and guys stepped off the court while making lewd and scurrilous remarks and vanished as utterly as if they had never been born, although you could hear their voices, amused and muttering, in the pines. And here and there, two or three times a game usually, a guy with a chest big enough to land a plane on would go soaring and sailing into the dark, leaping off the court and vanishing absolutely, except for a split second when you could see his sneakers hanging in the air like planets. That's all I wanted to tell you, just that.

In the Café Rue de Turenne,
Charleroi, Belgium, 1943

As soon as the German major entered the café, the manager was aware of the officer's slight unsteadiness and overexuberance; the major eyed the waitress slightly too long, shucked his overcoat onto his chair with a carelessness rare in an officer, and ordered not a glass but a bottle of wine, which the manager delivered himself. The major sipped the wine, pronounced it excellent, and then ordered without looking at the menu. The manager jotted down the order while noticing a yellow folder in the major's coat pocket; it had been jammed into a pocket slightly too small for it and it was buckled and protruding.

The manager poured more wine for the major, signaled for bread to be brought to the table, and went to the kitchen. In the kitchen were four people: the cook, a man of about forty; his teenage son, who did all the dishwashing; a man of about sixty who did all the heavy work, like lifting ice and unloading trucks; and the cook's other son, about age ten, who helped his father slice vegetables and prepare sauces. This boy, even at age ten, was wonderfully talented in the kitchen, and the manager had already let him make his own dishes occasionally; he had a lovely touch with soups in particular, and the café already featured whatever soups he chose to make. A bold move, to give a boy of ten his way in the kitchen; but these were hard days, and anything that would bring people through the door was a very good thing indeed.

The waitress came into the kitchen and saw the manager and understood.

We will have four minutes, no more, said the manager quietly. What he has must be important. The color gives it away. Give him another glass, without making much of the pour, and then he will visit the restroom. I will take the folder and bring it here. Each of you will have a minute, no more. When you hear the toilet flush, crowd the hallway a bit, to slow him down; and you, Justine, present yourself, and escort him back to his table. You might linger a moment or two, but don't sit down. Ready?

They all nodded, even the boy.

Justine and the manager went back out; just as they stepped through the door they saw the major drain his glass, and Justine, with the evanescent step of an experienced waitress, was at his elbow an instant later, smiling as she poured. The manager kept an eye on the front door to be sure the major was not expecting company. The major sipped from his second glass, and a moment later scraped back his chair and stood; he looked inquiringly at the manager, who nodded toward the rear of the café. As the major turned he clipped his overcoat with his hip, and the coat slumped to the floor like a shot animal. The manager, with the same practiced grace as Justine, was bending over the coat an instant later, and draping it back over the major's chair, brushing a shoulder of the coat with one hand. He then stepped into the kitchen. In the folder were two pages of typed sheets, each with the name of a city followed by a string of numbers; in all there were twenty cities, and twenty runs of numbers after them. He handed one sheet to the cook and the other to the man who did the heavy work, and then positioned himself by the kitchen door; Justine stood at the end of the little hallway that led from the restroom back to the café.

Just then a boisterous quartet of men at a table by the window actually shouted for Justine to bring them a second bottle; she delivered the bottle, opened it, evaded their favor, and was back at the end of the hallway in seconds.

In the kitchen the cook and his sons wrote numbers furiously into flour they had spilled and smoothed onto the chopping block;

the man who did the heavy work wrote his numbers into blocks of butter in the cold room. In both cases they wrote the numbers first and then the first letter or two of the corresponding city, not the whole name of the city; Na for Namur, for example, and Baa for Baastschnech. The man who did the heavy work somehow finished his page first, and handed it back to the manager; an instant later the cook's youngest son handed theirs to the manager, who put both pages carefully back into the folder and walked out into the café just as the toilet flushed. By the major's table he bent down to pick up the spoon he had left on the floor, and slipped the folder back into the coat just as the major stepped out of the restroom and found Justine smiling as she brushed past him. He smiled and said something complimentary and Justine bowed slightly in acknowledgment. The manager held the major's chair for him and an instant later the cook, with a flourish, delivered the major's meal. The manager filled the major's glass, looked at the nearly empty bottle with disapproval, and signaled Justine to bring a second bottle, on the house. This Justine did, and the major, after tasting his first bite and offering fulsome compliments to the cook, expressed his gratitude for the manager's hospitable gesture. The manager bowed slightly in acknowledgment and then stopped by the four men in the window to see if their meals had been satisfactory, which of course they were, especially the soup. The manager bowed slightly and said he would pass the compliment to the chef. The four men debated a moment about a third bottle; the manager leaned down and showed one of the men a particular bottle of German wine that he highly recommended, and the man stared up at him and nodded that he understood, and would be back later for the numbers. The four men then decided that two bottles were plenty and they had probably better be getting home, as the evening was growing late.

Mr Kim's Song

Weirdly enough the one time I was ever lured into a karaoke bar, by an office event I could not afford to miss, there in Room Two was Mr Kim, singing his heart out with the door shut tight. The way karaoke bars work is that you can either sing with other people, and laugh your ass off at how terrible or impassioned your companions are, or you can sing alone, for whatever reasons you want to sing alone, and there in Room Two, to my absolute amazement, was Mr Kim, singing alone.

The very concept of Mr Kim being in a karaoke bar was so wild and implausible that I went back to the door several times to be absolutely sure, and by God it was indeed Mr Kim, although he was not wearing his usual baker's smock, nor the black suit and black cap he occasionally wore if he was attending a wedding or a wake after work. He was actually wearing a tee shirt, which was unthinkable for Mr Kim; I was relieved to see he was not wearing jeans, which would have sprained my eyeballs permanently, I think. The shirt was outré enough; the very idea of Mr Kim in jeans, rather than his meticulous old man pants, as my kids called his pressed trousers, would fry the synapses of anyone who had seen the man week after week for many years in the bakery, as I had.

In a karaoke bar you can sing any of thousands of songs, for which a machine provides the music, and a large television screen scrolls the lyrics. I was most curious to see what song Mr Kim was singing with all his might—something from the old country, perhaps, which might give me a hint of just what old country Mr Kim was from, a question he never answered. A love song, giving a hint at who or what he loved? A drinking song, a country song, a glam rocker? But I could not see the screen from where I stood by the door of Room Two, and the booths were all soundproof. I could ask the bartender, perhaps—there must be a central console from which the owners or attendants could monitor the booths—but this seemed intrusive, even for a professional journalist, and perhaps there is a code of privacy at karaoke bars, for all I know.

But just as I stepped away from the door, surrendering all hope of ever discovering the song Mr Kim was singing, the door opened suddenly, and there was Mr Kim, glaring at me.

For those of you who know Mr Kim, you will know the weight of this moment; Mr Kim could be rude and terse and blunt and challenging at the best of times, and it was no stretch to imagine him vituperative and furious at having been seen in a private moment. But once again he did the unexpected—you never could predict or assume his behavior—and he gently took me by the elbow and drew me into Room Two.

You wish to know what song I was singing, I would guess, he said, and to my surprise and relief his voice was friendly and even gentle. I will tell you. Or better I will sing it again. It is the most beautiful song in the history of the world. I sing no other song. I sing this song when I am low and weary. It brings me back up to balance. It restores something in me. I would guess you know what I mean. I would guess there are songs like this for you. I think perhaps everyone has songs like this when they are low. You can sing the song anywhere anyhow of course but I find this way the best way, at least for me. Something about the amplification perhaps. Or the privacy. When you sing at home or in the shop people hear you singing and they think they know something about you from the song you sing, or something about you *because* you are singing, but this is not so. No one knows anything about anyone. We think we do but this is an illusion. It's just that sometimes all you can do is sing your song. So I come here to sing the song. You will not tell anyone about this. I am sure I can trust you to forget that we had this conversation. I do not need to bribe you with bread and pies. I will trust in your good judgment in this matter even though you are a journalist.

He spoke with a kind of honest passion I had not seen in him before, a sort of revelation that was highly uncharacteristic of him; he was one of the most private and tightly wound men I had ever met, despite his occasional silent kindness and generosity, which he would vehemently deny, for murky reasons, if you tried to thank him for it. I had seen this happen many times, and puzzled over it, but perhaps Mr Kim is right that no one really knows anything about anyone in the end; we get and give hints and intimations, and perhaps that is the best we can do.

I didn't say anything, there being nothing to say; and also I have learned, in my years as a journalist, that sometimes silence is productive, and not every lull in the conversation needs filling. Mr Kim stared at me for a moment, clearly mulling something over in his head, and then he said, Here, listen, I will sing the song, and then you will forget this conversation, and the song I sang, and the fact that I sang it. Now I know you are a journalist, and you will want to write this down someday, but I am sure I can trust you to not do so until I am gone, one way or another, either from life or from the shop. Put it this way: when you have no idea where I am in life or death, then you can write it down.

And with that he punched a button, and the music began—lean clean piano notes, but I could not place the melody—and then Mr Kim closed his eyes and began to sing. All the rest of my life I will remember that moment. Beyond all expectation, so far beyond imagining that the word shock doesn't even come close, Mr Kim had the most beautiful high liquid wavering shivering tenor voice I had ever heard, and he sang from the bottom of his soul, with every iota of his being. He sang the whole song through, as I stood there so moved I could not speak, and then he punched the button again, and the music stopped, and that was the end of that.

Sometimes even now, when he is long gone, his shop shuttered for a while and then leased anew as a jazzercise studio, I sometimes hear that song on the radio, or shimmering from someone's car, or even reaching out for me from a doorway; this last happened a few days ago, as I walked past a shop, and I turned and walked back and stood by the doorway, listening until the whole song was done. To my absolute amazement I found myself weeping.

> *I loves you, Porgy*
> *Don't let him take me*
> *Don't let him handle me*
> *And drive me mad*
> *If you can keep me*
> *I want to stay with you forever*
> *And I'll be glad. . . .*

Roma vs. Lazio

The archbishop, as per canon law, had mailed his retirement letter on his seventy-fifth birthday, a Wednesday. It arrived in the papal nuncio's office on Friday. Ordinarily the papal nuncio would have placed the letter, unopened, in his diplomatic pouch, and waited until Monday to send it to Rome, but he knew the importance of this particular letter, and arrangements had already been made to have it personally delivered, by a young monsignor, to the Vatican. The monsignor boarded a red-eye flight from Washington to Rome on Friday night, delivered the letter Saturday afternoon, and carried a reply—also prepared long before the archbishop had mailed his own letter—back to the papal nuncio early Monday morning.

The young monsignor and the papal nuncio sat for a moment in the papal nuncio's office, talking about the unseasonably warm weather in Rome, and the soccer standings: Lazio was ahead of Roma by three points, but the wolf will catch the eagle, as always, as the nuncio said with a smile; he had been a Roma man since he was a child in the streets, whereas the young monsignor, like many American prelates who studied in the city, had become a Lazio man, and even had a Silvio Piola jersey in his office. The papal nuncio had once had his secretary swap a Bruno Conti jersey for the Piola, and he and his secretary much enjoyed teasing the young monsignor that he had not noticed the switch for two days.

But that is the way with Lazio, who notices? said the nuncio.

Has he made this same joke fifty times, or sixty? said the monsignor to the secretary.

Anything else to tell me before you get some rest, my friend? said the nuncio.

No, Excellency, said the young monsignor. Everything was as you said, and there were no surprises. There was some discussion in the café about candidates for succession.

Betting?

More a discussion of possibility, Excellency.

You know the rule of thumb; any name mentioned aloud is reduced in probability by being spoken.

Yes, Excellency. You have pointed that out before.

Have I?

Yes, Excellency. And you have noted that the same rule applies to Americans who seek the Episcopal ring, that every admission of ambition dilutes your chances by half.

An ancient rule of thumb, so to speak, in the Church.

Yes, Excellency.

You did not have time for a soccer match?

No, Excellency. I thought about catching the second half of the Napoli game but Napoli is down in the cellar with Palermo and Genoa.

Probably for the best. You want to see Roma against serious competition. We rise to our best selves when we are challenged. When we are not challenged we grow stiff. We calcify.

There was some discussion in the café, Excellency, about how the archbishop was . . . challenging. I forbore to participate, of course.

Sensible. To join in gossip is never a good idea, and in Rome, well . . .

Yes, Excellency.

It isn't that he was *challenging*, exactly, said the nuncio. Challenge is healthy; challenge is invigorating, and even Mother Church needs vigor, needs young people like yourself. It's that he chose independence over the counsel of his superiors. Yes, yes, he made *motions* of respect to authority . . . is that how you say it? Motions?

Gestures, perhaps, said the monsignor.

Gestures of respect, continued the nuncio, but they were not genuine, he did not take to heart the counsel of even his fellow bishops, let alone the structures of authority here and abroad, and those are structures that have supported the Church since time immemorial, long beyond the memory of man. Is there not value beyond any one man's opinions in a structure that comes from Saint Peter himself?

Yes, Excellency, said the monsignor.

Granted, the man faced enormous problems, enormous stresses, said the nuncio. One would not wish such a load on any of our brothers in the faith. And he leaves the archdiocese back on its feet, back in good financial standing, and that of course is paramount, for what ministry can we possibly deliver if we have nothing?

None, Excellency.

Exactly so. Exactly so. So while one can admire his management of enormous problems, and salute his accomplishments after fourteen years, one must also question the manner of his administration. Did he in fact *embarrass* the Church with his public statements? Does what amounts to public confession and humiliation *advance* the Church or *detract* from our work?

A subtle question, Excellency.

Between you and me, my friend, this is why we have this letter from Rome sitting between us. A man who stands in the public square and says that the Church sinned, allowed sin, disguised sin, lied about sin, allowed and protected crimes, allowed and protected criminals, that is not a man who is advancing the work of the Church. That is a man who is *detracting* from the work of the Church. There are times to be transparent and times to work behind the scenes. He seemed to be of the opinion that to be transparent at all times was a good idea. Perhaps that is *not* such a good idea. One must consider the public relations, is that how you say it?

Just public relations, Excellency. You would say one must consider the weight of public relations, or the impact. Which certainly was considerable.

International! said the nuncio, with a rare emphasis. It is certainly true of the nuncio, as his secretary had often said to the monsignor, that he is a man of remarkable equanimity. He has never lost his temper that I remember, and not once have I heard him make a snide or rude remark, or raise his voice, even in the most private circumstances. A man of uncommon grace. That certainly cannot be said of me.

Nor me, the monsignor had replied, smiling.

Yet we must salute the man's sheer endurance, said the nuncio. Fourteen years, in the epicenter of the . . . problems. That is a terrible stress. Perhaps retirement will be the best thing for him. His health of course is Rome's paramount concern. He is no longer young.

No, Excellency.

Nor am I young, said the nuncio, rising from his chair. I am Roma, the ancient one, and you are Lazio, the rising one, and the future will perhaps be yours.

Rome is not to be questioned, it is to be loved, said the monsignor with a smile, also rising from his chair, and it took the nuncio a second before he got the joke, that this was Roma's team motto, and he burst out laughing and shook the monsignor's hand.

You could hear that laugh a million times, said his secretary to the monsignor, as she saw him to the door, and it would be just as infectious and joyful as the first time you heard it. One of the subtle reasons I am so committed to Our Holy Mother the Church is because a man like that is in charge. There are *so* many reasons to admire Our Holy Mother the Church, but the fact that a man of such subtlety and humor is in authority, perhaps that is a quiet miracle. So many people, even some archbishops, think they speak for the Church, and think they can say whatever they want about sin and forgiveness, but the fact is that really only a few people speak for the Church, isn't that so, Monsignor? Perhaps that's one of the quiet miracles of Our Holy Mother the Church, that someone is in *charge*, that wise men steer the ship. So very many things in our time are left to the will of the people, but there is no such thing as *the people*, there are only individuals with their own opinions, and not to be impolite, Monsignor, but how many of those opinions are uninformed, or worse? So when someone says that the Church sinned, and allowed sin, and protected sinners, and that these sins were also crimes for which the sinners ought to be jailed, and this same someone *apologizes for the Church*, and says he is ashamed of his Church's actions and inactions, and begs forgiveness from those who were shattered, even using the words *what we have done and what we have failed to do*, well, these are the opinions of one *individual*, even if he is an archbishop, and no one individual can speak so bluntly and not expect consequences, isn't that right, Monsignor? Isn't that so?

It's a very subtle question, to be sure, said the monsignor, and he bowed slightly, knowing that she loved that ancient courteous gesture, especially when offered by a priest, and walked back to the rectory. Just as he turned the corner by the restaurant someone opened the door and he heard a blast of familiar noise; it took him half a block to realize it was the roar of a passionate soccer crowd, and, considering the hour and the restaurant, there was a decent chance it was actually Roma versus Lazio, the wolf against the eagle. He thought for a moment of turning back but he was suddenly so tired he could hardly haul himself up the steps to his bed.

Dear Mum,

Good news: all charges were dropped. Bad news: we have to return both police cars. I don't like this arrangement either but I think we should, as you always say, look on the bright side of the street, which is where I found both cars. There they were, unattended and lonely, keys in the ignitions, windows rolled down, eager and authoritative, and The Brother and I, remembering your dictum that things should be used properly for what they were designed for, never for example use a rake to dig a hole or a shovel to diaper a child, acceded and acquiesced to what we considered to be an invitation, an act of respect for utility, an example of gratitude for the creativity of human beings, for what is a car but a remarkable feat of engineering and innovation? To invent an engine that harnesses tiny explosions and mills them into sustained energy driving gears with which to spin wheels, and the very wheels themselves wonderfully turned metallic discs lined with materials from the redolent islands of the Asiatics, well, a car, or two, is a testament to inventiveness, to the sort of thinking that has made the human being such a fascinating and in most respects positive and productive element of the evolutionary parade.

We made these points politely to the magistrate, but he seemed a dyspeptic fellow, not disposed to think creatively about ideas like communal property, public use of materials paid for by the public, occasions of spontaneous joy, acts of civil theater, the paradox of the words *speed limit*—as The Brother noted, eloquently, how can there be a limit on speed, the very word indicates untrammeled progress—but after our time with him we found ourselves not annoyed at his recalcitrance, Mum, but empathetic. One can only imagine what the poor soul must endure over the course of his working day, the scurrilous and scandalous, the connivance and crime, what rascals and raconteurs must scurry and shamble in his chambers, their stories mere shards of truth, draped in motley and shrouded in fog. As The Brother said it was our moral duty to elevate and entertain the moist little man, and do what we could to bring some light to the mordant stumble of his courtroom, as dank as a deacon's handshake.

Lovely cars they were, too, and as The Brother says we should be proud of our public defenders that they attend and maintain vehicles with such care and respect. The petrol tanks were filled, the interiors meticulous, the oil recently changed, the windscreens clean and bright, the newspapers folded, the pastries fresh, the handcuffs shiny, the radios and in-dash computers in excellent working condition. We had occasion, The Brother and I, to test the vehicles under the most adverse of road conditions, and I report with admiration that the handling, acceleration, balance, and braking capacity were, in a word, stellar. I am sure, as The Brother says, that you have here and there wondered, while filing your tax forms, if your hard-earned dollars were being well spent by those who represent us in the various closets of government, and I can say wholeheartedly that our police force has equipped itself with fleets of the finest automotive enterprises hatched in the minds of men. As The Brother says it was nothing less than an honor to be invited to operate such terrific manufacture.

So then, all's well that ends well, and once again hoopla dissolves like froth on the edge of the sea, and what is left, as you so often taught us, is an excellent story, or in this case two. For many years to come The Brother will be able to tell, with his usual high and winsome glee, of our chariot race from Sydney to Perth, at speeds hardly imagined by the visionary souls who built the steeds in which we flew like Mohammed to heaven, and I will take up the tale when he flags, and tell how we began with a shared impulse, a magic moment in the minds of men who shared your womb, but came finally, somewhere deep in the desert, as dusk sifted down and the stars awoke, to a timelessness, a great calm, a sort of wisdom, that had something to do perhaps with love, Mum, and maybe something more to do with those gargantuan extra petrol tanks under each car, you wouldn't *believe* how far you can go on your surplus tanks.

All our love, Your Boys

Mr Oleander

Mr Oleander was a thin slight man, perhaps sixty years old. He was a doctor. He was never seen in public without his hat. He had once run for mayor but had been defeated. He was respected but not revered or beloved; his manner was too severe and proper for reverence, and children as a rule disliked him. He had delivered more than a hundred residents of the town into the world and been at the deathbeds of a hundred more. He liked to joke that all he wanted from his medical career was to break even in the end. When he made a joke he waited slightly too long to deliver the punch line. He liked to make the same four or five jokes many times, each one suitable for its occasion. He considered himself a superb chess player and had been county champion in his day. As a chess player he was respected but not revered, and twice in recent years young challengers had arisen to nearly take his title in the town's annual winter chess championship. The annual winter chess championship was held in the town hall. Despite the plethora of modern media and the ancient game's slightly fusty air, the annual tournament still drew many of the town's young people; indeed this year more young people had entered the competition than ever before, and three of the four finalists were under the age of twenty, the fourth being Mr Oleander.

Mr Oleander had played steadily and conservatively, waiting with preternatural patience for his opponents to make mistakes, and then grimly making their error, however small, the hinge of his victory. The slightest slip was made to pay heavily: a careless pawn, an impulsive knight, a lazy rook. He played slowly himself but stared accusingly at his opponents as they sat thinking over their play; more than a few were rattled by his heavy gaze, and moved too quickly, and soon lost. But not his penultimate opponent, a young man named Naiman; this boy, perhaps twenty years old, stared so relentlessly at Mr Oleander as he played that Mr Oleander grew visibly rattled, and had to ask for a break, and then another, for the first time that anyone in the audience could remember. The boy Naiman stared so fixedly at Mr Oleander, in fact, that finally he moved his queen, instead of the bishop he had maneuvered beautifully to close a corner trap, and lost the game. He continued to stare at Mr Oleander, however, even as he left the stage, and would not answer questions about why in heaven's name he had moved his queen, was it an accident, was it a failed attempt at something deft and subtle, what?

The final match, on Sunday afternoon, drew an enormous crowd, nearly the entire town, including the small fishing fleet, or what was left of it in these years, as well as the whole police force, and all the religious professionals for miles around, and even some of the hospital patients with lesser injuries and manageable neuroses. And so many young people! So many teenagers and boys and girls in their early twenties were present that the town council put rows of folding chairs on the stage, also for the first time that anyone could ever remember; the younger people, being supple, sat on the floor among the folding chairs as well. No one could remember quite so many young people at the chess championship and the match judge in particular was delighted at the turnout.

The final pitted Mr Oleander against a young man named Avior, who was by some accounts sixteen and others eighteen. He had no father to speak of and his mother supported her two sons by raising and selling fruit from the orchard on which they rented their very small house. The boys were excellent students and very good with their hands, as you might imagine boys in a penniless orchard would be, so many things needing to be repaired, but they were both quiet, and neither was well known at the school, other than as good students. Mr Oleander, out of the goodness of his heart, had often stopped by the orchard and taken the boys for small adventures—to the beach, to the circus, to baseball games—and was especially attentive to Avior, probably because he was such a promising student, and might even become a doctor himself someday.

The game began so slowly that those who were not students of chess would think the players were conservative, but those who savored the game saw how closely matched the players were, and how the entire first hour of the game was essentially a test of vision and flexibility. Mr Oleander again stared at his opponent while waiting for his turn, but Avior looked only at the board, and rested his hand a full minute on each piece before he moved it. Avior leaned heavily on his pawns, moving them in ranks like a small army, while Mr Oleander slashed out occasionally with his large pieces, fending off pawns and trying to plunge into the heart of Avior's defense.

For the first hour neither player said a word, as is usual in chess, but just as the second hour began, and Avior, whose hand had been resting on his king's knight's pawn for a moment, moved it a single space from Mr Oleander's exposed king, Avior looked up for the first time and spoke aloud so clearly that people in the hall balcony heard him as if he was sitting among them.

The oleander, you know, is poisonous. We admire it but it is toxic.

Mr Oleander, who for once had been staring at the board, looked up, startled.

The flowers of the plant can change their colors, said Avior, to look much like flowers that are not poisonous.

Avior, we do not talk during a chess match, said Mr Oleander gently.

The fruit of the plant is long and narrow and releases many seeds in all seasons, said Avior. It does not adhere to the norms of behavior. It is aberrant. Do you know that word, aberrant?

What is this? said Mr Oleander, appealing to the match judge. What is this talking? He is trying to disturb my concentration. This cannot be allowed. I appeal to you.

Cultivars often use the word showy for oleander, said Avior, by which they mean it appears to be beautiful but it is a thin and shallow beauty. Again aberrant. Your move.

I know it is my move, said Mr Oleander angrily. I do not need you to tell me how to play the game I taught you. There, *there* is a castle for you to scale, you rude child.

The oleander grows everywhere and anywhere, said Avior, even more clearly than before, moving another pawn and trapping Mr Oleander's rook. It spawns and broods in every environment. Yet again aberrant.

He cannot talk! shouted Mr Oleander to the match judge, who adjusted her spectacles nervously. This is not allowed! This is not the way we play!

Your move, said Avior. What will you do? How will you explain the pawns who are no longer powerless? There are so many. We have strength in numbers. We have power, you know. It is a capital mistake to think that small things do not have power.

Why are you sitting there silent! shouted Mr Oleander at the match judge. And you! You are to be silent, boy! I tell you to be silent!

We were silent too long, said Avior. We did not know there were so many of us. But now we know. Now the pawns are coming for you. We will say aloud what you have done. We are saying it now. We are all here in this room today. Many of us are on the stage. I will speak and then another and another. I will speak of what was done to me and to my brother and to a dozen others. We will speak of it now so that everyone knows. A single pawn is powerless but many pawns are not. Your move.

There is my move! shouted Mr Oleander, slamming his king on the table so hard that it bounced fully two feet in the air and came down spinning among both players' pieces, knocking down enough pieces so that the game could not be reconstructed, and Avior was named the champion. In the newspaper the next day the account of the game said carefully that Mr Oleander had retired from the match, which was true.

The Mighty Currawongs

In recent months many fanciful stories have been told of the Mighty Currawongs, a new Australian Rules football club with offices and training ground in Box Hill, a suburb of Melbourne, the large southeastern Australian city where footy, as its adherents call it, was born in a paddock in 1858, rather like an ungainly colt. Having established its footing, the game, again like a colt, developed into a stunning combination of grace and speed, and soon took not only its native city but its home nation by storm; by the teenage years of the 21st century, there were footy teams in all corners of Australia, and a steady enough demand for the sport that there was a steady parade of expansion teams, of which the Currawongs were one. This note, then, is to correct some of the misconceptions about the Currawongs, and to set the record straight about the happy serendipity of events that befell the club, leading to its current popularity and unusually fervent fan base.

It was wholly by chance, for example, that the club's officials hired former Geelong Cats stalwart Cameron Ling as their first coach; Ling, after a stellar career in midfield for the Cats, with whom he won three league titles, retired just as the Currawongs finished planning for their opening season, and club officials, much impressed with Ling's work as captain and relentless defender, chose him to train their young players properly in the fundaments of the game. The first press releases issued by the club about this hiring, however, referred to Ling only as C. Ling, because, as it was discovered later, a public relations intern whose name has never been revealed, probably a Melbourne Grammar graduate, was unsure of the spelling of the name bestowed on Mr Ling by his blessed mother upon his moist entrance into this plane of existence in the winter of 1981.

Thus rose the waters of confusion, and became a raging flood, and did overflow the media, one member of which casually in a blog post bruited the opinion that the Currawongs, which he called the Wongs, were a Chinese team, just as, by purest chance, the first player promoted to the big club from junior football was the fleet and muscular Jason Yang, a lad whose grandfather hailed from the Pearl River delta in southern China, and the second, a tall boy built like a gum tree, was the now-renowned ruckman Kevin Kao. These signings, and the rumor that the Wongs were building a roster of Australian Chinese players, led to a stunning surge in season ticket sales among the Chinese community, in both the traditional hotbed centered around Little Bourke Street in Melbourne proper, and the outer populaces, notably Box Hill and Bendigo.

Yet another happy chance, an attentive player agent in Adelaide named Howard Lo who represented the talented South African prodigy Stephen Sung, brought young Sung to the Wongs, and Sung's signing ceremony, itself a memorable event to this day in Box Hill, led to the swift recruitment and signing of the rest of the now-famous roster: Han, Teng, Feng, Tung, Wei, Fan, Jen, Wan, Kang, Lin, Yen, Hou, and the older Tu brothers, not to be confused with their younger twins, who still may be swayed from their love of cricket to the beloved immense ovals on which Australia's national game is played.

At this juncture in the young life of the Mighty Currawongs the usual rabid bigotry poured forth as if from a wound that had not healed, notably the always seething Andrew Bolt, who raged and sputtered about invasions and secret agendas and pusillanimous kowtowing to political correctness, even going so far as to make a series of snide remarks about certain people being identifiable as evil by their small stature, until the now-renowned ruckman Kevin Kao paid a personal visit to the offices of the *Herald*

Sun, still a memorable event to this day in Southgate, where, according to some reports, the streets were lined with people cheering Kao's blunt insistence that in the Australia *he* loved and was born and raised in, a man's color and size and heritage had nothing whatsoever to do with his patriotism, integrity, accomplishments, and opportunities for career advancement, except perhaps in the ruck, where a certain burly alpinity, as Kao entertainingly told a reporter for *The Age*, really helps.

Many observers, in fact, point to this very conversation between young Mr Kao and *The Age* as the key moment not only in the nascent existence of the Mighty Currawongs but in the history and story of Australia itself; it was the e-magazine *Eureka Street* which perhaps most eloquently characterized the amazing events in the weeks following Mr Kao's striding along the Yarra River to "deliver the message of the real and best and deepest Australia," as he told *The Age*. The burst of street protests against racism in every corner of Australian life; the masks of every color that Australians from sea to sea wore on Michael Long's birthday; and the boom in stories from Australians of every color about their hilarious and joyous experiences with Australians of every other color finally put to rest forever the idea of an Australia riven by race. As the editors of *Eureka Street* noted, no force on earth can make us color-blind, for we are finally mammals of enormous sensitivity to otherness, having been trained over millions of years to trust only our own clan and suspect ill will of others; and while Australia since the moment of its founding as a mighty nation has battled racism against its own first peoples and peoples from Asia who once represented a bitter enemy in war, it is now as cheerfully eloquent, blunt, and pointed in international discourse about the savage idiocy and cruelty of racism, which costs not only untold pain and suffering among both haters and hated, but billions of dollars in lost time, creativity, and productivity at every level of society and commercial enterprise. Indeed it was the new prime minister Patrick Dodson who in a recent speech lauded the essential death of racism in Australia, credited the Mighty Currawongs for the precipitant incident in a truly remarkable moment in the long story of his beloved nation, offered the now-renowned ruckman Kevin Kao a position in the national ministry upon his retirement from football, and noted, to what can only be characterized as a roar of approval from Australians far and wide, that, with complete respect for the adherents and supporters of so very many football clubs around the nation, it was the Wongs for which every citizen barracked in his or her heart.

Jesus Joseph

Was the name of a young guy who showed up for practice one day
and no one knew who he was, but we were short a few guys with
twisted ankles and pulled hamstrings and such, so we let him run
with us, and he turned out to be, well, the Jesus Joseph that everybody knows now. You could tell after about ten minutes. He wasn't
a big guy, but he was wiry strong, had real quick hands and strong
wrists, and he could run all day. After the first hour of practice
you could also see that he was one of those guys who seemed to be
drifting but he would always be in the right place. I don't mean nec-
essarily where the ball is, but where the juncture of the play is, you
know what I mean? That kind of guy. He would just be where he
was supposed to be, having arrived there without apparent effort,
and he would make the necessary play without adornment, and
then he would drift away again to wherever he was supposed to be
next. It was fun to watch him once you got the right angle on the
way he played the game. There are lots of ways to play well—powerfully, deftly, furiously, theatrically, laboriously, dutifully, and some
more that I will remember if you buy me another beer—and this
kid played deftly, but usually guys who are quick and handy like
that are not much for crashes and collisions, and you can smash
them off their game with bad intent and the right angle, but not
Jesus Joseph, it turned out.

We usually practice hard for an hour, take a break, and then run
a light second hour, more to work on the legs than on our games, but

I remember the second hour of that first practice with the kid was intense. All of us had seen what he could do in the first hour, and a lot of guys, it turned out, wanted to make a statement or something, because one guy after another tried to crack him, to say welcome to the big leagues, or don't get cocky with all that talent, or don't forget who was here first, or something like that. But weirdly no one could quite nail him—you could get a hit on him, sure enough, but only glancingly, he would always spin at the last second, or another guy would get in the way, or you would stumble just as you were ready to lower the boom. It got funny after a while, that no one could really get a car crash on the kid. Even I tried, and I liked him already for the way he was quiet and shared the ball and didn't try to be the hero. But something about him also said *hit me*, and to my surprise a few minutes before we called it a day I took a run at him too, I got a good angle on him as he went up for a ball and I went in hard, but he changed gears at the last second and I clipped him rather than clocking him. The weirdest thing, I remember, was that I was angry that he got away. This doesn't make sense, and I feel like an idiot saying it here in public, but I felt it so strongly I still remember it like the taste of blood in my mouth. Weird.

After practice we all shook hands and introduced ourselves and said welcome to the club and stuff like that because it was quite clear without anyone saying anything that he was on the club now, and the club secretary, an old guy named Malcolm, got all his information and numbers and all that, and got the kid to explain his name, too, because Malcolm is a sharp old duck and he knew the media would seize on the name. It turned out the kid's mother was originally from deep in the mountains where the custom was that one son would be named for the Savior as a sort of living prayer or sacrifice or something. According to the kid his name was properly pronounced Hey Zeus, but Malcolm didn't like that and changed it to the usual pronunciation and hounded the newspaper and television guys about it. The kid just smiled and didn't seem to care about what he was called. Interestingly in the next couple weeks of practice guys tried to pin a nickname on him, which is an ancient habit in our sport, but none of them stuck, they just sounded forced or stupid, even ones that you would think might work like

JJ or The Kid or Jay Joe, so after a while everyone just called him Jesus with a smile, like you were also making a joke about his name while actually referring to the kid, like in interviews or something.

It's also interesting to remember that even while every one of us, and later guys on other teams, tried to clock the kid during practices and games, that everyone who was asked about him had only good things to say about him. It's the players who really know a guy, not the sportswriters and owners and fans and all, the players have almost a secret language of respect and disdain for other players, and while sometimes the media and fans will trumpet one guy, the players know that deep inside the game that guy is not as good as another guy who's not as flashy or talented but actually plays the game better. But Jesus Joseph was that rare guy who got nothing but respect from the players even while the media and fans thought he was the second coming of, well, Jesus.

You wouldn't believe the craziness, and how fast it came, and how high it built up, unless you were in the middle of it. I mean, everyone knows his name now, and something of the story, but those first few weeks, man—none of us had ever seen anything like it, and we were mostly veterans, and had played with and against some of the greatest players in the game. I am still not quite sure what made it all so different. A lot of reasons you *could* see and explain clearly, like he actually was an unbelievable player, and he was the nicest most genuine kid, and because he didn't talk much that actually probably fanned the mystery, and then there was his name, and the fact that no one had ever heard of him before he showed up for practice that first day, he wasn't one of those phenoms who get identified and trumpeted at age twelve and end up with blown knees and a cocaine problem by twenty. But the other things that made it such a mania for a while are a mystery to me. He wasn't real handsome, and he wasn't real quotable and funny, he wasn't one of those once-in-a-generation athletes that seem to have been sent from another planet, and he didn't have an irresistible story, like his parents were killed in the war and he survived in the jungle and learned to play by tossing coconuts around with the local primates. He was just an unbelievable player, in the end, and a real nice kid.

I should say something about him as a player, again from the point of view of another player. I think maybe something that fans and media people don't quite get like players do is that the game is like a language. Things are said and even shouted without words when you are inside the game. And it's not just your teammates. You get to know guys on the other teams real well just from how they play. I mean, you spend ninety minutes with a guy, at high speed, with everything on the line, pitting everything you have against everything he has, in what really amounts to a form of war, if we are honest about it—yes, you know that guy. Some guys you can't stand, some guys you have a grudging respect for, and some guys, on your team and yes, on the other teams, you are sort of just happy you were allowed to be on the same field as those guys. Guys like that bring some larger thing to the table, so everybody in that game is thrilled to be in it, even if you want to hit the other guy so hard his eyeballs fall out. I don't have words for this larger thing I mean. I have been thinking about it for years now, and I still don't know quite how to catch what I mean. A sort of generosity, maybe; and some kind of odd joy. Put it this way, every time I played a game or even a practice with Jesus Joseph, it was a deeper game or practice, you know what I mean? It was harder and more intense, but more . . . electric, somehow. Like it meant more, even though it was just a game.

I am not explaining this very well and I better go back to the story. Well, the kid was an immediate superstar, as you can imagine, and by the end of our first regular-season game he was on the front page of the papers. It went wild from there. Servers shut down and computers froze because of the kid. Every ticket to every game was sold out in five days and our television presence tripled. By our third game our games were on cable and satellite all over the world. I kid you not—I remember a story that showed red dots for every country where you could turn on your screen and see Jesus Joseph, and the planet was one huge red dot, man. By the third week our practices were sold out. By our sixth game, according to another story, we had been watched by more people than had watched all the games in the sport in the whole history of the sport. I don't tell you this to boast; I just tell you so you get a sense of the thing. It was crazy time.

But also the same thing I noticed in our first practice was now happening constantly in our games; the other teams were obsessed with running Jesus Joseph. And again some of the reasons are simple: in every sport if you can get the other team's best player out, you have a better chance of winning; in every sport clocking a star is a crushing psychological blow; in every sport a kid running wild and free is an affront to the older lesser players, who naturally get a little resentful, not to mention we are not stupid and we see our jobs and money and careers running by us with a smile. So I know a lot of the reasons guys busted their nuts to smash the kid.

But I keep thinking there was some other thing going on that again I don't have good words for. It was almost like the kid was such a good kid, such an unbelievable player, so genuine and unadorned, that you wanted to punch him in the face. Like his good made you feel bad somehow. This is a weird line of talk but me personally I think it's the only way to understand why guys were so intent on running him. Even I felt it and I liked that kid more than any other kid who ever walked onto the field with us and picked up a ball.

By our ninth game things had built to such a frenzy that a lot of guys on our team were spending more time punching out guys on the other team who were trying to crush Jesus Joseph than we were trying to win the game. It wasn't that we were so aggressive; it's just that you can't let a guy run a teammate without delivering a warning to that guy, and when a guy doesn't get the message, eventually you change your delivery method, to quote an old coach of mine. After that game we had a team meeting and decided to move the kid back on the field for his own safety; fewer guys would try to run him, we thought, if he was on defense, and he was such a gifted player that we figured he would stop as many goals as he had scored, so we would all be square. But this didn't happen. In our next few games teams spent even more time trying to smash him back there, and we spent so much time trying to defend him that we were not scoring, so finally our coach decided, with our blessing and the kid's, the put him back at the head of the snake, and trust that his eerie timing would keep him safe, while also bringing back the usual barrage of goals.

There's been a lot of talk that what happened is the coach's fault but I want to make it clear that we all agreed on that decision, including the kid, and it's another compliment to him that if he had the slightest inhibition about the move, it wouldn't have happened. Believe me. If he had even cleared his throat and hesitated an instant we would have clapped him on the back for being an honest dude and gone back to playing him on the back line; we had that kind of respect and, yes, love for him. I am using the word love here on purpose. Sometimes you need to use the right word for the right thing and this is one of those times. If you are the kind of reader who sniggers and makes a joke here, screw you.

He got crushed, sure he did. It had to happen sometime; I can't sit here and say with a straight face that it's conceivable the kid could have played ten or fifteen seasons, even with that eerie timing, and survived hundreds of great players trying to break his bones. But the weird thing is that before it happened we actually did think, deep in our hearts, that he could do that. We thought he could do anything. We saw him do anything he wanted. We saw him do everything we knew was possible in the game and things that were impossible. We saw him do things that no one had even imagined could be done. *And he didn't do them for himself*, that was the deep thing that was the most amazing. He did them because they were fun, because they made us better and deeper and joyouser, as my old coach used to say. In a real deep way I think he did those things not to win the game, or for our approbation, but because he loved the game and wanted to respect its untouched imaginative possibilities, and because he loved us. The one time I ever saw him laugh out loud in a game was after one of those things, he made a play that literally cannot be made, not just athletically but because you couldn't dream such a combination of skill and imagination and verve was possible, and while he scored on the play, and it was actually a crucial goal, he ran back toward us not with neck-vein-bulging triumph but with a face like a little kid who just saw a whale for the first time, sort of thrilled and delighted and amazed all at once. I tell you, the kid, for a moment, for all that he was muscled and famous, looked like he was about seven years old in that moment. I'll never forget that moment.

In our last game that season, late in the first half, he got crushed. I still don't know if he didn't see it coming, or if he was shaking off the rattles from a whole half of near-death experiences, or if maybe he just let it happen for some weird reason. All I know is that I was about ten yards away, and saw him go up for the ball, soaring up without the slightest effort like he did—that kid had the quickest hops I ever saw, it was like he didn't even have to bend his legs or take a step before he was six feet up and rising—and then I saw the other guy coming like a laser beam, and most of me almost smiled because I had seen this before a hundred times and it was fun to watch the kid just sort of step aside as the bull roared by raging, but a little part of me saw the angle and was afraid. I am telling you the truth here and not trying to be the star witness or anything. I think it was that I have played the game so long that the angles and geometry of it are in my brains like calculus equations, and even though I had seen the kid avoid this same crash for a whole season, a little part of me, the cold math equations part, couldn't see any way he wasn't going to get hammered this time. And, God help me, just this once, finally, he caught the railroad car full on, right in his chest and face, at the highest speed a guy can achieve in this game, and with bad intent, which adds another ton of collision juice.

It was a clean hit. I said that to the referee, I said that to the match judge, I said that at the inquiry, I said that to the media, I have said it for years to fans at autograph shows and reunions and benefit dinners. It was totally clean and fair and part of the game, even the bad intent. I have hit guys with bad intent myself many a time and I don't feel bad about it and I have even privately said to the guy who hit Jesus Joseph that there's no reason to feel bad. He lined the kid up and clocked him, and that's part of the game, and it's not his fault the kid, for once, didn't slip the noose. In a weird way I think the guy who clocked the kid has been vilified for the kid's own genius at not getting hit, you know what I mean? Because the kid never got hit before, by all those opponents

and yes, by us, furious and cruel, in practice, the one time he *did* get
hit resounded way more than it would have if the kid was a player like
the rest of us.

The rest of the story is the usual thing, that was the kid's last
game, he never again walked onto a field and picked up a ball and
grinned and said *mind if I run with you guys?* The media made a
huge deal out of his retirement for a while but a couple of years
later the kid was basically just a glowing footnote. I am writing
this mostly to try to catch some things that should be said about
the kid before they get forgotten but there's one last detail that
probably explains it better than I could with words. In the two
years after the kid got crushed, a whole lot of guys retired seem-
ingly before they should have according to the usual calculations.
There was only one sportswriter who noticed this, that I remember,
a guy named Flanagan, but I think those guys, me among them,
stopped playing because the game was shallower without the kid in
it. I loved the game, and I loved my teammates and the competition
and the money and the kick of being a little famous, but I found
that even in the middle of a heated playoff game it wasn't the same,
and I discovered that I didn't want to play the game if it was never
going to be that deep way again. When the kid was on the field
with you or against you, there were like extra doors you could run
through, something like that, and to know those doors were closed
was too much. I talked to a lot of the guys who retired around the
same time as me and you would be surprised how many guys used
sort of the same kinds of words to explain why they couldn't play
anymore. Guys tried to be polite and articulate and say the usual
things, like they couldn't play at the level they were accustomed to,
and they felt their skills were waning, and they didn't want to cheat
the fans they liked and respected, and they wanted to spend more
time with their families, but you would be surprised how many
guys mentioned the kid in their last press conferences, and talked
about the kid when we got together for reunions and benefits and
stuff like that. More than once when I was at a benefit dinner and
we were sitting in a corner afterwards with beers talking about the
game we would end up talking about the kid, sometimes for hours.

So in a sense you could say that the kid is still playing, because I can tell you for a fact that a hell of a lot of guys have spent a hell of a lot of hours talking about being inside a game with the kid, which was an experience unlike any of us had ever had before or since.

The Detours

Some years after I played the trumpet poorly in a jazz band called The Lucid Moments, I was recruited to play in the horn section of a band playing summer dates on the New Hampshire coast. This was a ska band, at least for that summer, and while it had various names depending on what kind of music it was playing, for that brief beach tour it was The Detours, which had been one of the early versions of The Who, a band we all worshipped.

One of the great things about playing in a horn *section*, rather than just playing the trumpet all by yourself on stage, is that you can hide in the tide of brass, which I did happily for each of the few dates we played as The Detours. We played bars and pubs, we played two festivals, we played one grand opening of an automobile lot, and we played a show at the Club Casino in Hampton Beach, and it is this last show that I wanted to tell you about, because somehow it caught every single part of what happens when a band catches fire and the audience is open and ready, and also somehow it is what I think of when I think of the word summer. You'll actually see and *feel* that night, if I can tell it right.

First of all, it was a hot night—late in July, when the summer has gathered all its force, and grown to full maturity, and you know it will be like this for only another week or two, and then it's all downhill to September and school and work and sleet and fistfights over your parking spot. The boardwalk was packed, the beach road was filled with cars cruising slowly past the big green signs that said ABSOLUTELY NO CRUISING, and the *smells* in the air . . . man, it would take me a week to list them. Fried dough, suntan lotion, exhaust, hot dogs, stale beer, mustard, fish, spilled soda slowly fermenting under the boardwalk, slightly too much perfume from Massachusetts girls, slightly not enough on Maine girls . . . maybe very faintly you could smell baseball gloves and fireworks and oil on boats and ships. And you could hear the Red Sox game on the radio, and car horns, and laughter, and maybe gunshots in the distance, and the squeal of tires, and the ping of pinball machines, and the chink of money, and the rattle of old engines, and whiz of zippers, and the roar of cassette decks, and the tattoo of high heels, and cheerful lies of every sort, from *the first one is free* to *I will love you forever.*

Second, we were playing the Club Casino, and those two words are always spoken in italics, you know what I mean, the *Club Casino*, because that place is a shrine to *something*, man, it's a huge old wooden pile of a building that has seen and hosted and housed everything you can imagine over the years, from roller derby to boxing, from weddings to shootouts. The good sweet Lord alone knows if some activity known to man has *not* occurred in the Club Casino, because everything you and I can think of between us certainly has. I am not kidding—go ahead and propose something crazy, you'll see what I mean. Parking planners convention? Happened. Dog races? Happened. World harmonica championships? Happened. Memorial service for sailors who only spoke Portuguese who were lost at sea? Happened. Trust me when I say that the Club Casino is like the center of the world, and there we were, The Detours, just a ratty little temporary ska band from Boston, tuning up on stage of the *Club Casino*. If you read this in a bad novel on the beach you wouldn't believe it, right? But—it happened.

Third, the crowd was *huge*. I mean, it was beyond huge. It was beyond sense. I can't imagine that more than fifty people there that night had even heard of us, let alone ever heard us play, but there were two thousand people there officially, that being capacity according to the fire marshal (who was there, and roaring drunk, too), but I think there were more like *three* thousand people there.

I mean, there were people on *stage* with us, that's how crowded it was. And people standing dense against the old wooden walls, and people hanging over the balcony, and people so thick and jumpy in front of the stage that the floor was shaking. It was wild. I never saw a crowd like that before or since. Certainly that's because what dense crowd would come to hear a band I was in, right? But still, you would not *believe* this crowd. Close your eyes and imagine a huge dark room absolutely throbbing with people, most of them half-drunk and itching to dance, on the hottest wildest night of the summer, in a place where summer was probably *invented*, and that will give you a sense of what we saw from the stage. As our drummer said later it was like being on a boat in the middle of the wildest sea you ever saw in your whole life and it was terrifying and thrilling in about equal measure.

We figured we would start with a bang and then ease up in the middle with some ballads and slower stuff, but we never did slow down, probably because all of us knew that if we slowed down at all the crowd would tear us limb from limb, so we started at a hundred miles an hour with songs by The Specials and the Beat and The Skatalites, and then sped up for some Madness songs and two from The Bodysnatchers, and then we really went deep for some Ernest Ranglin and Dizzy Moore and The Blues Blasters, and by then we were exhausted and sweating so thoroughly I thought we were all going to get electrocuted right on the stage, but by now the crowd was in such an uproar you couldn't hear yourself think, and so we just kept playing faster and faster. We were running low on material, though; one great thing about ska is that all the songs are three minutes tops so you can play a whole set in an hour, and we usually topped out at about an hour, but this night in the Club Casino we shot right past an hour like a bullet, and we played every other song any of us could think of, we got so where one guy would just start into a song and the rest of us would pile on as fast as we could play, trying to figure out the changes on the fly, and another great thing about ska is that you can do that, you can start playing at a million miles an hour and then sort of surf along crazily behind the leader, and this is what we did for a while, playing mostly songs by The

Paragons and The Dragonaires, until finally not even our singer, who was totally deeply madly into ska history and knew such lost souls as Judge Dread and Baba Brooks, knew where to go next.

But listen, before we finish our set that night in the Club Casino, I want to spend a minute reveling in the epic incredible roar of it, the absolute bonkers noise and joy and bouncing around. I was not kidding when I said the floor was shaking, and it was more than shaking—it was sort of seething, like a tidal swell, and I swear the old wooden walls *shivered*. People were jumping and dancing and crashing into each other and the waitresses were half-scared and half-laughing and the bartenders and bouncers were yelling but you couldn't hear anything at all coming out of their mouths, and all the people on the stage with us were jumping up and down, so that the stage was also shimmering and shivering, and we were playing so loud and so fast we lost track of what song it was. For the first and last time in my musical life, such as it was, I wasn't playing a song, I was just *playing*, you know what I mean? We had arrived at some sort of place that I did not know you could get to in music, and I am pretty sure I will not ever get there again, not in music anyways, but rather than being sad about it, or feeling like I lost some cool thing I'll never recover, I feel totally lucky that I tasted it once.

I have often thought, in the years since that night, that this feeling of being completely immersed in something that was scary and ecstatic at the same time is a feeling that you get in other aspects of your life—I felt it here and there as a basketball player, and I felt it when I asked my lovely bride to marry me, and I felt it when our kids were born—and there are days when I think that this feeling is sort of the deepest human feeling we get, you know? Maybe a great deal of what we talk about when we talk about God and holiness and epiphany and satori and enlightenment and love is that feeling, thrilled and terrified and fully completely utterly aware that for this moment you are equally close to both epic disaster and epic levitation as you are ever going to get on this planet. You can see how some people would get addicted to trying to get that feeling all the time—I think maybe that's what's up with extreme sports nuts, and rapturehead musicians like Van Morrison, and some people who really get into drugs—but I wasn't a good enough trumpet player to think that moment would ever come again for me musically, which is maybe why I have remembered that night so clearly, and why I don't want this story to end.

But we had to finish sometime, for any number of reasons, like not getting thrown off the stage by the seriously enormous bouncers, and we were out of songs, and we were so soaked and drained I think we each lost five pounds that night, so we played one last song, and by chance, or maybe not by chance, we picked exactly the right song, the Skatalites' "Freedom Song," which is a long jazzy riff without words, and we played the hell out of it, with every last drop of energy we had, but we slowed down as we went along, until by the end everyone got the message, that this had been an incredible night, and we should all cherish and remember it until the day we died, and we should sip these last few minutes and savor every last drop. Right near the end of the song there's a break where each horn takes a run and then falls silent, and I was last, and I remember when I finished I stared out at the crowd, and people were swaying and smiling and some girls and even some boys I could see were crying. When we finished there was a crystal silence for about half a second and then the place went so bonkers I thought the ceiling was going to fly off, but it didn't. After a couple of minutes the lights snapped on and the bouncers pounced like linebackers and that was the end of that.

We did two more shows a week later up the coast but they were little venues with no advertising to speak of, so hardly anyone came, and then summer ended and the band dissolved, which is what happens to bands, you know, they don't last, bands are affairs and not marriages, even dinosaur bands are together only for money and not for the kicks, and even dinosaur bands in which the members dig each other, like the E Street Band, have to keep replacing and regenerating parts, so that was the end of The Detours, but no one felt bad about it, and no one even suggested reconstituting the band hoping for another night like that night. I think for once everyone understood that something cool had happened that you could not call back or command. It was enough that it had happened once, for no particular reason, and that a lot of people one night in the Club Casino understood and savored the fact that it had happened.

Right about here in a story the writer usually finishes with a thoughtful remark, or says something wise and sidelong, but I am not a writer, so I will end like we did that night on stage, by just smiling and walking off. Thank you and good night.

Chauncy Street

Many years ago when I was in my twenties I worked for a small and obscure newspaper on Chauncy Street in Boston. The newspaper office was also small and obscure, as was Chauncy Street itself, which began forthrightly enough at Summer Street, one block north, but then petered out indeterminately once it crossed Essex Street, one block south, where it either became silent partners with Harrison Avenue or was *subsumed* by Harrison Avenue; you couldn't really tell, no matter how many times you walked slowly south looking for the exact spot where Chauncy Street vanished as if it had never been born. It was that kind of street, brief and mysterious, as were its commercial enterprises, few as they were. There was a coffee shop on the corner that seemed to change hands every three months, though it never changed its name or menu or denizens, and there was a large vacant lot toward Summer Street where gulls and crows bred pigeons for market, and there was the newspaper office, where one of my colleagues actually wore a fedora hat with a press pass in his hatband, and another drank copious martinis at lunchtime, and there was a tailor, a man as brief and mysterious as Chauncy Street itself.

His name was Sachiel, he told me, which means the angel of water, and he was all of five feet tall, perhaps, and nearly five feet wide, a square of a man; he essentially filled his tiny storefront, which could not have been more than eight feet wide and eight feet deep, although the ceiling inside was so high you couldn't see the end of it from the street, which is where all Sachiel's customers stood, conducting their business on the bottom half of the shop door, which Sachiel used as a work-table. He sat behind it quiet as the Buddha, moving only his hands, although there must have been times when he reached for, or even unimaginably *climbed* for, some of the incredible welter of buttons, needles, thimbles, bolts of cloth, scissors, tape-measures, shears, rolls of thread, and bottles of lotions and integuments that filled every inch of his space and probably dangled from the unfathomable ceiling. I wonder now if he did most of his work at night, when the door was closed, clambering up into the far reaches above, which may for all I know have risen endlessly from his closet of a storefront; but work he did, for whatever day he had promised you your renovated jacket or resurrected shirt, it was ready that day, not only meticulously repaired, but cleaned, pressed, and folded into neat packets made from folded newspapers.

It was one of these newspaper packets that deepened my conversations with him, which had begun on a purely transactional basis. One spring day he returned my only jacket to me, a sad garment the color of sacrificial calves, and the wrapping, I noticed, was the sports page of a newspaper I had never seen, called *Ha'aretz*. Being a newspaper man, albeit a dewy one, I assumed this was a neighborhood paper, Boston being so rife with tiny papers at the time that even the gulls and crows in the vacant lot toward Summer Street had a small trade paper filled with articles about market fluctuations, and Sachiel, smiling like the Buddha, said indeed it was a neighborhood paper, from his old neighborhood to the east.

Now, even I, young as I was, knew there was no east to speak of from where we stood, the only east any further east of us being the islands of Boston Harbor, where no one lived unless you were fleeing the law or the lawless, and when I pointed this out to Sachiel he smiled and said he meant even *farther* east, in a land where he had once been a boy "headlong as a hawk and twice as hungry," as he said.

"I was perhaps a third of the man I am now, so to speak," he continued, his hands showing me the lean eager boy he had been, "but I was so restless I could never stand still, let alone sit, which is perhaps why now it is the other way 'round for me, so as to achieve balance.

Which also may explain why I am now in a city, because for the first twenty years of my life I lived in a dense forest of cedars, enormous and ancient trees, some of which had seen saints and angels, and were marked as such by those who had eyes to see the signs. There were owls so old in that forest that they remembered the days when lions and ostriches roamed the plains down below us, and it was said that there was a kingfisher so ancient near a spring high in the mountains that he could no longer fly or see the things of this world with his eyes, and was served food and news by troops of thrushes and woodchats, and protected by a praetorian guard of masked shrikes. This was how my childhood was, filled with animals and stories of things no one knew but my brothers and me. But then came wars, like immense animals no food could satisfy, and we had to leave our forest, and were flung upon the wide world like tiny birds caught in a tempest. Each brother went to a different country, where he found the work he was marked to do. It took me many years before I discovered my work, but now that I know what I am to do, I do it with joy, even though I have grown very old and very fat, and soon I will be gone also, and my shop unmarked and unremembered. I tell you now that someday you will walk this street and look for this shop and there will be nothing here at all, no door and no memory of a door, and no mark or sign of a man whose work was to stitch the world back together after it was shattered into uncountable pieces. It took us many years before we discovered our work, but my brothers and I did find what it was we were to do, and each of us stitches as much and fast as we can before we are taken by the angel, but we are told by our youngest brother, who was chosen as a messenger among the worlds, that we are very close to finishing our work, and we will be returned to our blessed forest, in some way or fashion we do not know. To me this is joyous news, and this is why, my young friend, you see me smiling, even though I am very old and very fat, and seated in a dark cave in a dark street in the city. Here is your jacket, which I must say is also very old and will not last much longer, even though I have done what I could do for it. Now I must get back to work. I hope that you find *your* work, and do it well, before you are taken. Sometime before winter you should stop in here again and let me repair your pants. Do you have a second pair of pants? You work for a newspaper, do you not? So you do not have another pair of pants. I have several pairs of pants here that have been abandoned to me by their previous occupants. Choose among them as you like, and come back here before winter. Perhaps there will come a day when you have done your work well enough to own a second pair of pants. I hope that day will come. Do not be greedy and ask for more than two pair of pants. A man needs only two of everything. More than that is unnecessary. Remember to come back before the winter."

But when I came back that autumn, after the first scatter of snow reminded me of winter and his instructions, indeed his shop was utterly gone, the gleaming wall of a new hotel having taken its place, and there was no mark or memory of the two halves of his door, one which swung open and the other which served as his work-table; but he has not gone unremembered, as you see, for I wrote this story, and you read it, and perhaps somehow he felt what we have done together, which is another way to stitch together what was unraveled.

Guys Who Knew Guys

Brian Doyle, bowing in memory of the inimitable late George Vincent Higgins, Esquire

I knew a man who once actually said to me, at eleven in the morning, as he was drinking a large glass of excellent red wine and smoking a cigarette under a sign that read ABSOLUTELY NO SMOKING, that he knew *a guy who knew a guy*, which was a phrase I had read in crime novels but never actually heard spoken seriously, which it certainly was here; the guy who said it had devoted years as an assistant district and federal attorney to catching and imprisoning *guys who knew guys*, as he said, and he spoke of these guys with a deep and abiding distaste. We were supposed to talk about literature during our conversation but we never really got around to it because he got so annoyed talking about guys who knew guys that he had a second glass of wine and another ten cigarettes and pummeled the subject so bluntly and colorfully that I never forgot it. Why anyone ever wrote a book or made a movie or a television show about these clowns is a mystery to me, he said. They are merely thugs. They are unbelievably stupid and cruel thugs. They are not funny. They are not amusing. They are not comical. They do not have a code of honor. They are not guardians of their neighborhoods against the ravages of official corruption. They *are* corruption. They are slime bags. They are dumber than rocks. They would kill their own children without blinking. They have done so. I could tell you stories. They would rat anyone out so fast you couldn't write the ratting fast enough. I have had a guy yell at me for not writing fast enough how many guys he was ratting including not one but two of his own brothers. They have no friends. All they have is money, temporarily. Mario Puzo, he should rot in hell for making them popular. Francis Coppola, too. A million stupid kids thought being a thug was cool after *The Godfather*. I spent thirty years stuffing them in jail as fast as I could and I would have happily dropped them all at the bottom of Boston Harbor except the harbor is already polluted. Best place for them would be Greenland or something, drop them on the ice and let them eat each other. Listen, I listened to thousands of hours of recordings and I know what I am talking about. In one of their clubhouses we put so many bugs there were more bugs than chairs. These guys are dumber than fruit. Their idea of a sophisticated operation is knocking over an ice-cream truck, which they have done. They have actually stolen candy from babies. They have stolen pets. They have stolen Bibles. One guy stole a car and locked himself into it and couldn't get out and couldn't get it started and finally he called the police. Another guy stole a greyhound dog and the dog attacked him relentlessly and he called the police also. Are you getting the picture here? Half these guys if you told them their last name they would have to check their wallets for their first names. Half these guys if you gave them five dollars and asked for change they would give you ten. The king of these guys in New England when I was working was a guy in Providence who was such a thug he stole money from church baskets. I kid you not. This guy had his own brother killed. This guy ordered a father to kill his own son. This guy beat up waitresses. Where is the part where this is funny or amusing or comical? I missed that. Mario Puzo gets to be a millionaire for telling stories about these guys, and Francis Coppola gets to be a millionaire for telling stories about these guys, and I spent twenty years catching these guys and throwing them in jail and getting death threats and *almost* making enough money to pay the mortgage and *I* don't get to be a millionaire. Maybe *that's* the amusing and comical part. Maybe that's the lesson. You invent thugs, you get rich; you chase thugs, you get dead. But hey, I got a million stories from my years. I can dine out on my stories. Like today, am I right? More wine?

Elson Habib, Playing White,
Ponders His Opening Move

He considers opening with the queen's pawn, remembering his grandfather's rules of thumb. Open with a central pawn, Elson. It does not matter which. Cease your pawns after two or at maximum three moves. Bring knights into action before bishops. Bishops are sly and should be held in reserve. They are not to be fully trusted. There is a reason they move in a sideways scuttle. Do not let your queen travel freely early in the game. She should be held in reserve for the moment when her power is revealed. There will be a flash of glory. The woman is the warrior. The king is a poor creature. Castle him as soon as possible, preferably with the rook on his side. You must protect him but do not ring him too close with soldiery or he will be trapped. They will betray him. This is the story of the centuries. Play for the center. Feel free to develop your own openings and wing play, however. I am just your first teacher. I am only an old man under a tree in an alley. Rooks are fascist. They only think in straight lines. But they have great range. They are hawks or falcons capable of a sudden strike after brooding on their cliff-face. Remember that the knights are your dearest friends. They can do anything and go anywhere. The most beautiful game entails dovetailed knight play and then the swoop of the queen. I saw a game like that played once in Aleppo. Everyone applauded after the coup de grace and the man who lost the game kissed the hand of the man who won the game. This was also a game played outside in an alley. Perhaps the fresh air stimulates the brain. This could be so. Endeavor where possible to play your games outside, Elson. Do not play for money. That is disrespectful. That is what men in Marseille might do, not us. Play for dignity. Play for memory. You would be surprised at how play stimulates the memory. For example I play the fianchetto and immediately a wonderful player from Alexandria comes to mind. He played his bishops like crossed swords. They dashed here and there with abandon. A most creative player. Now there was a man who would have been happy with fewer pawns in the way of his sprinting bishops. He would sacrifice pawns on purpose sometimes to set himself an imbroglio. This was his fatal flaw. A confidence perilously close to arrogance. Of this beware. One must be confident or you will accomplish nothing, yet there is a fine line between confidence and arrogance. The shadow-line, as Conrad called it. By all accounts an excellent chess player. So many writers were. Nabokov. Ambrose Bierce. Vonnegut. Raymond Chandler. Edgar Rice Burroughs. Perhaps the best chess players who were also writers were those who were exiled, or felt so. Or I play Alekhine's gun, with the queen lurking behind the two rooks, you see, a stacking of enormous power, and instantly there is your uncle Pavel, in his charcoal-gray coat, drinking endless cups of tea as he played, and slurping his tea most vociferously from the saucer, an eccentric custom. Deplorable. Perhaps that is how a man drinks tea in Marseille, but we know better. Once embarked, you must loosen your mind. Allow your memory to flourish. Imagination is the great secret of chess, not experience. This is why a young man like you can beat an old man like me. Your brain is closer to the source. Remember what I teach you but do not hold it close. The past is a teacher, not a master. Every game ever played is unlike every other game ever played. No two games have ever been exactly the same. Is that not amazing? I knew a man once in Ajaccio who believed that this was ultimately the reason we play the game at all. It is refreshing and stimulating to be presented with familiar things in new and interesting poses. In a sense the game reflects this world. I do not mean metaphor or allegory. Those are weak props suitable for men in Marseille but not for us, Elson. I mean moments like this one exactly. An old man sitting at a rickety table in an alley plays a tall smiling young man a game of chess. The old man has the highest hopes for the young man in very many aspects of life, but rather than lecture the poor boy at tiresome length he prefers to couch his affection and love in the language of the game. The young man understands this, and reads between the lines when his grandfather talks about such things as the primacy of imagination and the way a chess player must be intent and relaxed at once. The young man understands what the old man is saying to him in the words between the words. Similarly there are squares between the squares on the chessboard. Strive to see those subtle squares and bring your men to bear upon them. I knew a man once in Valldemossa who was a genius at that. He was both a dwarf and a priest. A most interesting and thoughtful man. He was of the opinion that the world was composed of spaces between and among the spaces, and that perhaps there were spaces between even those spaces. We use words like atoms and quarks for this sort of thing but they are only words, Elson. Words are like the principles and tactics of chess, good things to know, easy to hand, but finally mere means to ends, not ends themselves. I say this with the utmost respect for words. I knew a man once in Ullapool who was the most fluent and eloquent man I ever met, and I have lived a very long time. In the end he was stricken by an illness which silenced his tongue, a turn of events he found amusing and instructive. As you might imagine he was a wonderful chess player. We would play outside when practicable, which is not often in Scotland, but glorious when possible, that wild slanting northern light. He massed his pawns like herds of tiny arrows and sent them flying at the target of his choice. So when I say do not expend more than two and at most three moves on your pawns as you begin, remember my friend from Ullapool, and loosen your imagination, and play as you will. Speaking of which, it is your turn, and has been for some time now. Do not be distracted by the chatter of your opponent, even if his talk is as interesting and stimulating as mine. Do not be distracted by the songs of birds and the infinitesimal murmur of the train. Do not be distracted by sudden quiet remarks such as I love you dearly, Elson, and I hope that you will always remember these moments under the sycamore tree in the alley, when you and I sat across from each other, and played the greatest of games, as the blessed light fell down on us like golden dust, and the city murmured in our ears, and somewhere there was the burble and prospect of soup. But we will come to the soup when the time comes for soup, and that will not be until the game is finished, this game unlike any other game ever played. Rushing through a game to arrive at the soup may be something for men in Marseille to do, but that is not for us.

Elson Habib, Playing Black, Ponders the End Game

His grandfather died, as he had always said he would, in the café on Via Raffia Garzia, just after his first coffee, his newspaper folded crisply into quarters and parsed so that sports preceded news and opinion, as was only right and proper, Elson, as he had said many times, you want to have your comedy and tragedy delivered as unadorned as possible, and sports, which is as liable to be corrupt as any other human pursuit, is nonetheless not generally as cynical and laden with lies and flimflammery as the capering of politics or the devious trickery of commerce, not to mention the orotund *dichiarazione* of the ostensibly wise, which was how his grandfather talked, with amusement but penetration, smiling but sharp-eyed, amused but not foolish.

The men of the family handled the business details of the death, the women of the family handled the funeral and feast, and Elson, being the only grandchild, was sent to his grandfather's apartment, *to secure the room*, as his oldest uncle said, a phrase that made Elson smile as he walked down Via Enrico Besta, for he well knew that his grandfather would have made wry remarks about this phrase, *secure the room* from what, Elson? The ravenous wind? Tardy assassins? The ravages of time? The weight of sadness? What does your uncle, my beloved second son, imagine there is to steal among my effects? The only objects of value to me there are the ones that are of no value to anyone but me; other than the chess set, which is a lovely thing and no mistake.

And it was the chess set that Elson looked for first, when he stepped into his grandfather's room. Such a small room, but airy and shot with light; his grandfather had chosen it carefully, after his wife died, because it was at the top of the apartment building, with a view of the sea, but he did not have to climb the stairs, as the building was tucked into a hillside, and he could take the longer way around, which was a gentler slope, and enter his room from the back; indeed he had finally had Elson remove the front door of his apartment altogether and replace it with a large carving of the Madonna, on the theory that a door that was never used was not really a door then, and who could object to seeing a portrait of such a fine woman, rather than a drab entryway? And the chances are excellent, Elson, that she was a wonderful chess player, given her patience and wry wit. It is said that chess was invented in India after she ascended into heaven, but who is to say? Are there any newspaper stories from the day that chess was invented? No? Well, then. So to have a portrait of a fine chess player there instead of a door makes good sense.

Everything in the apartment was exactly as his grandfather had left it when he walked to the café, and Elson sat down, reverent. The small clock carved from wood found at sea. The silver mustache brush, older than his grandfather. The four coffee cups and four wine glasses; fewer vessels would be rude, Elson, and more would be unrealistic, at my age. The one hundred books exactly; one *needs* only a hundred books, my boy; the trick is to choose carefully which books are your companions; many people simply *accumulate* books and do not read them, whereas a discriminating soul has fewer books in toto but swims in them regularly; and the best books bear rereading, for somehow they always contain surprises and lessons you did not notice in previous readings. It is possible that some very good books continue to write themselves after they are published, perhaps working with their companions on the shelf, which is why I rearrange them twice a year, so as to provide them with new stimuli. Who is to say that they do not communicate among themselves, in ways only they know?

The chess set was open on its small oak table in the window. Elson remembered making the table with his grandfather when he was ten years old; they had worked on it all summer, making it from holm oak from the northern end of the island. As neither of them knew how to make a table, they had accepted the advice of a carpenter, who showed them how to carve and plane the wood, and join the pieces, and shave and sand it, and finally polish it with various oils, to protect it from the ravages of time, and to allow the wood to return the sunlight it had received over many years, as the carpenter had said. Wood is generous that way, the carpenter had said quietly, if people would allow it to be.

To his surprise Elson saw that a game was underway on the board, and he sat down to gauge the play. He sat in his usual seat, of course, and saw that he was playing black, which was unusual, as his grandfather had always given him the first move; the privilege of youth, the wage of age, Elson. But here his grandfather had opened with sharp play along the wings of the board, bringing his knights and bishops charging out of the back row, and putting black on his heels for several moves; yet black had deftly recovered his equilibrium, and now dominated the center of the board with his pawns, and, interestingly, his queen, which had leapt off the back line almost as soon as the game had begun.

Elson stared at the game for a while, soaking down into it, as it were, marshalling his concentration, forgetting that he was supposed to *secure the room*, instead probing the mind of the player who had sat across the table so many times, including this last time; and he realized that his grandfather had begun this game for him as a message, a letter, a gesture. Elson slowly played the whole game in his mind to the point where his grandfather had risen from the table, moving each piece slowly with his eyes, even mentally leaving his hand on each piece a full minute, as his grandfather had taught him; and when he got to the game as it had been left suspended, he realized it was his move.

Slow down, Elson, his grandfather had said many times when he was a child learning the game. Always look at all your pieces. Do not fixate on one idea. Be open. Extend the reach of your mind.

There are always possibilities that you do not see immediately, no matter how experienced and intelligent you are. No one is always in command. Remember that your pawns are powerful. Do not imprison your king and queen among their own courtiers, for they are easily trapped there, ostensibly under protection but actually helpless. Even if you are absolutely sure of the action you wish to make, pause and contemplate. Consider my pieces also. Imagine what I am after. Imagine you are the person across the table. Yet do not assume anything about me; that is the road to ruin. Instead study my play. I am what I do, not what I seem to be. Do not seek pattern, which leads all too easily to assumption and overconfidence and arrogance. Assume nothing. Whatever you are sure about, do not be. The game rewards attentiveness. It rewards dreaming. The point is not merely to win; victory is a byproduct of playing well. To win without playing well, or being challenged to play well, is to drink from an empty glass. The highest achievement is a game in which both players are playing imaginatively and at various levels of attentiveness. A game like that is worth more than victory. A game like that *is* the victory. A game like that is a way to say things for which we do not yet have words. Chess is a language. It is very ancient. It is also said that it was invented by a god in the forest, or on the beach during the siege of Troy. I believe on the beach during the siege of Troy. It is not a forest game. It is a game of light. It is good to play it at least by a window, as we do. Sometime there will come a day when I cannot play, for one reason or another, probably because I will have expired in the café on Via Raffia Garzia, but when that day comes, for even I cannot live forever despite the evidence, I will know it is the day of my expiration from the moment I open my eyes and am informed of the day's plans by the Madonna, and I will leave a game for you to finish, because you are my beloved boy, and I have never enjoyed playing chess with anyone as much as I have loved playing with you, and I have played with some extraordinary beings, yes I have. But none so extraordinary as you, Elson. None so extraordinary as you.

Elson stared at the board, and let himself soak further down into the game, and he forgot the ships moaning in the harbor, and the thrum of traffic, and the peal of bells, and the shouts of vendors, and the scream of brakes, and the groan of trains, and the shriek of gulls, and after a few moments he saw how to drive inexorably with his queen at his grandfather's king; and although his grandfather played brilliantly in riposte, parrying left and right and sending his knights and bishops leaping across the board like tiny tigers, Elson patiently pressed forward, until finally his grandfather stood alone and proud, and could do nothing but lay himself down, and expire.

Elson kept his hand on the fallen white king for a full minute; and then he laughed aloud, at the sheer beauty and verve and imaginative zest of the game; and then he wept from the bottom of his soul.

Her Kid

It came as a shock, although God knows why it would be a surprise, said her dad quietly in the kitchen as he and her mother processed the news at the little table in the nook. Her mother took a second to catch the nuance of his remark; she had been remembering how their daughter used to sit at this very table when she was small, first with three telephone books and then with two and then with only one telephone book, mama, I am growing *up*!

Well, said her mother after a moment, what do we do about it?

We? said her dad. We? Is this our decision, then?

I certainly think we have a role to play, said her mother. If only advice and counsel.

Or money, said her father.

Or money, said her mother, staring at him.

And indeed the decision did entail money, which her dad took care of, not even pretending to complain or jest, for once. All four biological parents and one second spouse weighed in, with no one making righteous political or religious speeches, thankfully, and everyone was so reasonable and solicitous; the fact is, the meeting went about as well as it could have possibly been expected to go, as her mother said later, and she meant it.

All five parents were also very impressed with the boyfriend, who accepted full responsibility, and took full part in the decision, and apologized in person to her parents for his carelessness. He even offered to be financially responsible for addressing the problem, as he phrased it, and while this was a mature thing to say, the parents agreed, the young man was not in a position to be of much actual help in addressing the problem, and so he was absolved of financial responsibility, although both dads made a point of telling him they were grateful for his offer.

After the procedure everyone was even *more* solicitous and kind and generous, if that was possible, and both mothers stopped by every day. Although no one was supposed to know about the procedure, not the housemates or brothers or sisters and grandparents or friends, a few people did stop by with casseroles and lasagnas and cookies and baskets of tomatoes; enough food to feed the whole house for a week, which thrilled the housemates, as they were all on the usual college student budgets which left about eight cents a day for actual honest food. The tomatoes were especially welcome, as there is no food quite as delicious and evocative and savory as late summer garden tomatoes, eaten moments after they have been picked.

Her mother got her up and walking as soon as possible after the procedure, and you would be startled how fast the weight fell off. They started with gentle strolls around the block, graduating to longer walks to her old elementary school and back, and finally they did the whole long walk to the river and back, at which point her mother figured everything was back to normal.

Although, I tell you, her mother said to her father in the kitchen the next morning, at the table in the nook, I couldn't *believe* how sentimental and nostalgic I was, walking past the grade school with her. Everything's *exactly* the same. There's the soccer field, and the swings and slides, and the monkey bars, and I just had such a weird time flip in my head. Two minutes ago we were walking her up to kindergarten and now we were walking . . . well, you know.

The next day she was back in class and back on her regular academic schedule, having only missed a week of school, amazingly, and the college was wonderfully solicitous about the missed time, providing free tutors to help her make up the work, and graciously accepting a letter from her doctor about her emergency medical situation.

I was impressed enough with that school, said her father to her mother in the kitchen, but now I am *really* impressed.

The boyfriend, to his credit, stayed in the picture; so very often something like this breaks up a young couple. He was in touch with her every day, with at least a text or a tweet if not a letter or a phone call, and they made plans for a long weekend skiing, just the two of them, to relax after such a stressful time, and to get back in touch romantically, after everything that had happened. The other biological dad, in a courteous gesture, booked their ski trip for them and quietly paid for everything, even a romantic dinner at the inn.

So in the end, said her mother in the kitchen one morning, at the table in the nook, that all went about as well as it could have been expected to go, all things considered. So many things could have gone wrong, but it's all taken care of now, and no one's life was ruined, and no one shouted or raged, and everyone got along. That went well, it really did.

Except for her kid, thought her dad, but he didn't say it.

The Mermens

Here are some things we thought were true about members of the Church of Jesus Christ of the Latter-day Saints, which of course we knew not one such person, growing up in a Catholic enclave in New York City where spotting the occasional Lutheran was a weekend sport, and there was rumor of a Jewish temple somewhere in Brooklyn, and one time the brother of a friend had seen a Hindu man on the street, or so he said, but he was not the kind of guy you could totally trust when he said that, and he may well have seen a rodeo rider, or a Mohammedan, as my grandfather used to say. We thought, first of all, that members of the Church of Jesus Christ of the Latter-day Saints were called Mermens, as my grandfather said, so we thought that members of the Church of Jesus Christ of the Latter-day Saints were an aquatic people, for reasons that were murky, considering their long affiliation with Utah, which we didn't think had an ocean, although perhaps it used to when my grandfather was young, which is when your man Abraham Lincoln was president, as he said. Also we thought-heard the Church of Jesus Christ of the Latter-day Saints as *Ladder*-day Saints, which was puzzling, but not even my grandfather knew what that was all about; it had something to do with Jacob's Ladder, he said, which we assumed was a town in Utah. Also we thought that members of the Church of Jesus Christ of the Ladder-day Saints had to marry someone new every other week, which would lead to a *lot* of wet towels left on the bathroom floor, wouldn't it, Brian? as my grandfather said. But marrying more than once was not wholly unknown in our Catholic world; Mrs Cooney, over to Saint Rita's Parish, had married Mr Cooney after the death of her first husband in the war, so she was both a widow and an adult, said my grandfather, who informed me helpfully that as a female adult she was what you would call an adultress. My grandfather was a font of such wisdom. Also he said that the Mermens had learned about football from the Catholics, who invented it at Notre Dame, and the Mermens were doing pretty well at the game, what with all the kids they have what with all those marriages, said my grandfather, the story is their first kid has to be a bishop or scout leader or something, and the second through fifth kids are trained to football, something like our system, in which a Catholic family produces a priest or a nun, a cop, a teacher, and a soldier or a sailor, after which the rest of the kids can be whatever they want, even Lutherans, in some cases. Also we thought the Mermens were pretty brave, all things considered, to send their kids two by two, dressed so handsomely in their white shirts and ties, into pagan neighborhoods like ours, why you Catholic kids never dress as well as the Mermens is a mystery and a disappointment to me, said my grandfather, those brave Mermen kids go right into the belly of Catholicism on their bicycles, and even their *bicycles* are dignified unlike those silly Sting Rays *you* kids ride, said my grandfather, and those poor Mermen kids must get laughed at or worse all day long, knocking on doors of people who will mostly say vulgar things to them, but they never reply rude as far as I can tell, which you have to admire, you wonder if Catholic kids in the same position would use the foul and vituperative language I have heard you and your brothers use, which I will not tell your mother about if you will be a good boy and go get your grandfather one of those cigars your grandmother has for unknown reasons forbidden in the house. She can be a stern woman, your grandmother, bless her heart, but you cannot hold it against her, because her great-uncle married a Lutheran, you know, and they are a stern and demanding people, given to nailing their opinions on church doors, ruining perfectly good wood. You wouldn't see the Mermens hammering their opinions on a beautiful door, no, you wouldn't. Fine people, the Mermens.

The Stigmata

October. Patient is forty years old. Caucasian male, Catholic priest. Heartbeat sound, blood pressure normal, slightly underweight for height. Complaint: pain in hands, feet, and lower left abdomen. Symptoms first manifested five weeks ago. Patient thought nothing of it, chalked it up to encroaching age, entropy, etc. Pain in abdomen increasingly severe however and during visit today patient was scanned for appendicitis, colon blockage, hernia, etc. No evident cause found. Patient sent home with ibuprofen. Patient noted that he was probably pregnant and this is what happened when there was a little too *much* Marian devotion but no one had ever told him of the dangers of such etc.

November. Patient returns complaining of sudden temporary bleeding from hands and feet. Says "wounds open for a few seconds and there is a trickle of blood and then wounds close again." No skin trauma evident on scan. Abdominal pain continues but no bleeding reported from inguinal area. Refer patient to Psychiatric Services for workup. Patient says he *knows* this all sounds pretty bizarre, he considers it *more* bizarre than any bonehead doctor could ever possibly imagine, he is a serious *stu*dent of bizarre, being a professional in the Church E*ter*nal, but the cold fact of the matter is that his hands and feet are bleeding, usually in the mornings, and he doesn't see exactly where a discussion of his complicated childhood or construction of social persona is going to do anything particularly helpful when it comes to mopping blood out of his socks before the housekeeper sees it because if Mrs Shea sees blood there will be chaos and hubbub which is not what he needs at this particular moment if I know what he means.

December. Patient reports that now a wound opens briefly in his abdomen and bleeds at the same time that the wounds in his hands and feet bleed, which is a bit of a problem, he states, when you are in the confessional or conducting a funeral or speaking to the fifth grade about the difference between the Gospel of John (mad poetry) and the Gospel of Matthew (fussy reportage) and that he is deeply sick and tired of the whole bleeding thing, clearly this is some sort of stigmatic experience which he doesn't want and doesn't think very helpful in the modern Catholic world anyway, it's a vestigial medieval thing that has to do with miracles having to be proof of faith, but that of course is nuts, faith is faith, that's all, you're in or you're out, it's not provable, it's a greedy thing to want proof of God, and besides all the proof you could ever want is all around you, duh, you want proof of the Coherent Mercy check out a sparrow or Mrs Shea.

January. Patient spends most of his visit talking about his housekeeper, although as he says it's not like there's much of a house to keep, I mean it's not like I am having wild parties every night, and when I am not sentenced to rubber chicken dinners celebrating the fourth-place finish of the parish volleyball team or such, then I lead a quiet life except for this stigmata thing, which finally boiled over when Mrs Shea discovered I was (a) doing extra laundry and (b) enduring ecstatic episodes during which I actually *hear* light, it's hard to explain, something to do with auras and voices and revelation and suchlike. Patient scanned again for any evidence of wounds or scarring on hands, feet, and inguinal area. None found. Psychiatric Services contacted again for referral. Patient says it's about time he cashed in his chit with the head doctor whereas this whole stigmata thing is cutting into his bowling schedule in a most distressing fashion and it's all he can do to get out of the rectory to go bowling because Mrs Shea thinks he should go exactly nowhere until he has healed and she is a forceful and remarkable soul.

February. Patient reports that among the voices he has heard is Catherine of Siena, who has, he says, a voice like a broken whiskey glass, and who told him that she had regular conversations with God, who *didn't like to be interrupted*, is that hilarious or what! The Lord of the Universe is a monologue guy like Leno and Letterman! Patient spent much of the rest of his visit roaring with laughter. Patient again scanned for "wounds" and "stigmata" and other skin trauma but no evidence found. Patient says symptoms are lessening as the world and Mrs Shea yearn toward Easter. Patient says against all evidence light will defeat darkness, hope defeat despair, love defeat death, etc. Referred to Psychiatric Services again.

March. Patient reports that while he still has cyclic pain in the affected areas there have been no bleeding events, probably, he says, because his body lives in mortal fear of Mrs Shea's formidable and forbidding glare, you wouldn't wish a glare like that on even an assistant pastor, and the glare she emitted like a laser ray when she found out about the extra laundry was a thing to behold and that's a fact. Patient reports that while he still is subject to sudden epiphanies and attacks of joy, they no longer knock him to his knees, which is a good thing because baseball season just started and once again he has to coach the Bantams and dropping to your knees during the game is considered bad form by coaches from the other parishes.

April. Patient reports that Easter healed all pain and sadness and his lower abdominal area. Scans are clean. Psychiatric Services report says no unusual conditions evident, just usual muddle and tangle of human condition. Patient spends most of the hour regaling nursing staff with stories of pastors he has known. Also went off on long riff about Mrs Shea, who is all things considered he says a fine and wondrous woman, donating long hours of her time to the upkeep of the pastoral residence, in which dwells the lowest of men, a servant of the faithful, not fit to wash the feet of the parish, all of whom, taken as a whole, are his fellow conspirators in the most countercultural and revolutionary idea in the history of human beings, when you think about it, eh, doc?

The People of West Kalimantan vs.
the Glorious Kayan Warriors of Borneo

I'll tell you a story. My friend Dickie was once taken hostage by revolutionaries in Borneo, and the way he tells the story is that the whole thing was like one of the old great Woody Allen movies, before the Woodster got all neurotic and obsessed with adultery and blind rabbis and people with English accents humping each other while waving tennis rackets.

The revolutionaries, says Dickie, were mostly teenagers, and all they did was eat and watch television, and a lot of the reason they took him hostage, he thinks, is that he had major cable access, and while ostensibly they were imprisoning him in his hotel room, and barricading themselves in with motion-sensitive bombs, and making rabid incendiary political statements to the media through cell phone and internet and telephone, really what they did was flip through the cable stations so fast that they eventually burned out the remote control and Dickie, who was a software engineer, had to fix it with a battery from his phone.

Which pissed me off royally, says Dickie, and finally we had it out, me and the leaders, who were these two pimply rockers with tattoos of Elton John, can you believe it, what kind of stoner idiot would put a drag queen on his body forever, you know? Gives you a sense of their priorities. Anyway I finally dropped the bomb on them, and pointed out that technically they couldn't rebel against the government of Borneo, because there *isn't* a government of Borneo, there are *three* governments in Borneo, the island's divid-

86

ed up into parts, they'd have to pick *one* to rebel against, so which one would it be, or is that too complex a decision for stoners with gay piano players on their arms?

Well, that set them off howling like Levon Helm, says Dickie, and they even turned off the cable for a while to have it out. Some of them wanted to rebel against the government of Brunei because it was the smallest, and some picked the government of Malaysia because they didn't like the colors of the flag or something, and one guy, who needless to say was one of the stoners with Sir Elton on his arm, wanted to rebel against Indonesia because they had a weak-ass soccer team that hasn't qualified for the World Cup since before he was born, and I didn't help matters at that point by encouraging them to rebel against the Malaysian government of Borneo because that was the government that once encouraged the parachuting of 14,000 cats into the country, true story, I always thought that must have been one of the great governmental meetings of all time, you know, the deputy minister for cats making a considered motion and the prime minister agreeing cautiously after conferring with his aides, you know, and then probably taking a break to go hump somebody waving a tennis racket.

Anyway, says Dickie, teenage revolutionaries have the same attention span as regular teenagers, which is to say zero, and the argument quickly shifted back to the television, some guys wanted to watch soccer and some guys were desperate to find the pornographic channels, and right about then the police finally gained access by pretending to be room service guys bringing burgers, so that was that, and I was left with a really messy room and no battery for my phone, but I got a good story out of it, right? And the end of the story is that because this all happened in the city of Kendawangan, which is in one of the Indonesian provinces of the island, the Indonesian government asked me to testify against these guys, but I just could not stop laughing at the idea of Sir Elton John in the dock, so I had to plead diplomatic immunity and the necessity for geopolitical secrecy and all that, which was a crock, you know, but I think it did help reduce their sentences. I did ask my staff back home to intervene and make sure the teenagers were held in a low-security prison in Teluk Batang where, bless my soul, there is cable access, so there you go.

The Lutheran Minister's Daughter

Her name was Fairly, which she also spelled Fairlee and Fairli, and which people misspelled in every sort of way, like Fairley and Farley and Fairy and Ferry, and of course her brothers called her every sort of mangle of her name, Furry and Flurry and Fatty and Flatty, mostly from affection but sometimes not; one of the first things she learned as a child was that even people who love you are more cruel than they know. Even her mom made edgy remarks, a little, as Fairly grew absolutely stunningly beautiful like her mom used to be; and even her dad, although he swore by the word of the Lord, which word, if you boil the whole New Testament down to a single word, would be Love, which is an idea that doesn't seem to include snide remarks to your beloved daughter, but it seemed that he could not help himself, occasionally, probably because he was worried that her beauty would be a curse, although he felt his flaw and regretted it.

Her dad had certain firm concepts of how things were supposed to be religious-wise, and Fairly did not often fit those concepts, and so there were long weeks when they were tense, and did not speak to each other, and he would go off fishing and hunting with the sons, or on trips of preaching and mercy with his wife, leaving only money under the fruit bowl in the kitchen for Fairly, not even a scribbled note. He kept hoping she would come around religious-wise, his phrase, but by the time she was seventeen he was weary of waiting for her to be what he expected, and just then she began to date the Catholic doctor's son.

The Catholic doctor's son was a burly young man who played football and read Walt Whitman and saw Fairly as a remarkable force of nature unsure as yet of her talents and how they might soon be effectively wielded against the ocean of greed in this bruised world, and he thought that when she got a good grip on her tools she would be a holy terror glorious to witness. Also she was just absolutely stunningly beautiful, and being with her was like being in bold italic type, as he said to his friends, who stared at her in amazement, wondering how a town like theirs could have produced such a startling verb of a woman.

The minister, upon discovering their troth, forbade and dissuaded, waxed wroth and fulminated, denied permission and issued punitive measures, but the years of mere money under the fruit bowl proved insuperable, and she too took to fishing and hunting with the Catholic doctor's son, and trips of preaching and mercy, for both of them were serious about the power of the Word, having survived mere religion to discover the deeper music in the life and work of the One; and both of them proved to be articulate and passionate messengers, blessed with patience and genuinely curious about the sea of story in every being. By the time they were eighteen they were renowned all over the northeast parts of the state, welcomed everywhere, asked to speak, the stars of sermons and Sunday supplements, and men stopped her father in the street to shake his hand and laud the manner in which he had led his daughter to the Light, which now shone from her countenance with a brilliance no star could match.

But her father wept at night, and confessed to the One that his own pride held him back from loving his final child as she was, rather than as he had expected her to be; and not until the day his wife led him to the river, and laved his brow, and spoke quietly, saying *embrace what is*, did his struggle ease, and a sweet stillness return; and from that day he was the father he wished to be, in whom witness is paramount, and expectation merely a memory. To his wife and sons he seemed quieter, more liable to humor, a man granted more hours in the day, and those more musical; and while he still fished and hunted for the table, he traveled less and listened more.

At the end of the summer of their eighteenth year the girl went west to college and the boy east, and they parted gently, for each by then knew the face of the future; the Catholic doctor's son became a priest, charging like a fullback at pain and despair ten months a year, and vanishing into the northern mountains every summer to drink of the waters of the One; the Lutheran minister's daughter became a teacher, and her village in the mountains near Canada built her a schoolhouse of cedar and pine, set against the hills where hunters occasionally saw wolverine and the last of the great bears for which the town was named. Every summer she went home for two months and walked with her mother by the river, and sat with her father in his study, and sang in the streets with her nieces and nephews, and read letters from and wrote letters to the doctor's son, letters composed only of the notes of songs, or drawings of fish and ferns, or maps of the patient stars. If we can use the word love in its largest and most wonderful sense, that being a generous tent so incredibly capacious that we cannot see or feel or conceive any limitation to it, one of the words we use for this tent being God, then we can say that she loved the Catholic doctor's son with every fiber of her being, and he loved her; and as the years went on they loved each other more, for while the world saw a love without the salt and swing of their bodies, they felt a love that deepened and expanded in ways they had never imagined possible. Some years they never exchanged a word at all, but sent each other the smallest of gifts, each eloquent and miraculous: a feather that fell into his hand, a pebble given to her by a child, the worn wooden prayer beads that his father carried on his rounds. When each of them heard the crunch of the postman's boots on the gravel leading to their doors, their hearts leapt; and both postmen came to realize their mailbags were filled with prayers beyond calculation or measurement.

The New Bishop

On August 1, feast day of Saint Alphonsus Liguori, the new bishop assumed his office, giving a most peculiar speech, in which he noted that he was absolutely certain that he, like Saint Alphonsus, would eventually be deserted by most of his companions, excoriated for abandoning pomposity for simplicity, and have his neck bowed by the burdensome weight of circumstance. He added that he too had asked that the complex penance of the bishopric not be laid upon his shoulders, weak as his shoulders had thus far proven to be, but such deliverance was not his lot, for which he asked the prayers of the faithful.

Bishopric? said people in the pews. Is that a word?

Ten days later, on August 11, feast day of Saint Clare of Assisi, patroness of laundry workers, the new bishop sold the phalanx of washing machines and dryers in the rectory basement. On October 28, feast day of Saint Jude, patron of lost causes, he sold the rectory's entire supply of bingo equipment, card tables, poker chips, and roulette wheels, some of the tables tracing back to the establishment of the parish itself just after the Civil War. On March 9, feast day of Saint Frances of Rome, patroness of cars and drivers, he sold all four of the rectory's cars, including the Buick on which Mr Mooney had worked so long and assiduously, buffing and revving, polishing and priming, shining even the various small bobblehead statuettes on the back shelf that *some* bishops, as Mr Mooney said, the ones with hints of senses of *humor*, had allowed him to install.

Those were the days, said people in the pews.

On March 8, feast day of Saint John of God, patron of booksellers and heart patients, the new bishop had a quiet heart attack while reading John Steinbeck's masterpiece, *Sweet Thursday*. He joked to his doctors that he would have never had a heart attack quiet or otherwise if he had not been reading the greatest of Episcopalian writers, who famously while an altar server at Saint Paul's church in Salinas, California, dropped a cross on a bishop's head.

I should have anticipated a blow to the bishopric, said the new bishop.

On March 19, feast day of Saint Joseph, patron of shelter and buildings, the new bishop sold the rectory itself, all ten adjacent acres including sheds and the former stable complex, and all attendant woodland except the dense grove of cedars at the very top of the hill behind the rectory. That parcel, approximately an acre of forest that had never been logged, was preserved by trust in perpetuity, and granted public access by way of the footpath that was annually cleared by the Boy Scouts as a community service project.

Is he going to sell the church itself, then? said people in the pews.

The rectory staff, generally advanced in years but quietly provided with complete health care and healthy pensions by the bishop with part of the proceeds from the rash of recent sales, retired, and mostly arranged to live with their children, although Mr Mooney, disgruntled, to say the least, moved to another island and offered his services to an Episcopalian parish led by a man who sometimes wore a BOSTON COLLEGE POKER TEAM sweatshirt, which Mr Mooney did his best to ignore, feeling that even the Jesuits had a place in the Church Eternal, as did, of course, the poor Episcopalians and their ilk, still smarting over the sins of the Church many centuries past, though those days were long ago and far away, and the whole idea of Protestantism being somewhat quaint, what's to Protest against, with the Church being the poor shaggy thing it is today, exhibit A being this new fella selling off the place lock stock and barrel, I ask you that?

Mooney has a point there, said the people in the pews.

The new bishop himself took up residence in a sorry little lean-to of a beach cabin near the Rocks, close enough to the church that he could walk back and forth or even God help us all ride that little green wisp of a bicycle he found at the Goodwill, and it must be said he was indefatigable on that thing, rain or shine, visiting each and every one of his congregation during his first year as he said he was going to do, you have to pay the man his due for that, said people in the pews, and he did indubitably bring back many of the lapsed and fallen, and draw a startling number of new congregants, mostly the young couples and their first babies, who caused a racket and no mistake, and the bishop closing the crying room and welcoming the squirmers and toddlers up front to crawl around the altar like it was a beach and him the sea.

Is the Mass a kindergarten project or what? said the people in the pews.

On September 27, feast day of Saints Cosmas and Damian, patrons of surgical procedures and organ transplants, the new bishop donated a kidney to a twelve-year-old female member of the parish and bone marrow to a nineteen-year-old football player at the local community college. The boy, who then recovered amazingly from his illness, was Episcopalian, and joked to the local newspaper that he never expected Catholicism to save his life. The newspaper had a field day with this and the story was picked up nationally, with a photograph of the boy in his football jersey holding a rosary.

On October 8, feast day of Saint Luke, patron of artists and painters, the new bishop sold all paintings, statues, carvings, sculptures, stained-glass windows, furniture, pews, rugs, candelabra, and fixtures in the church, holding back from sale and auction only crucifixes, the tabernacle, and the altar itself, a beautifully worked slab of cedar. The crucifixes were distributed to various parish homes, the altar was trucked to a barn near the beach, and the tabernacle carried in procession from the echoing church to the barn also.

Hardly a soul behind the new fella, said the people with no pews.

On January 31, feast day of Saint John Bosco, patron of boys and children and juggling and humor, the new bishop gave a most peculiar speech, in the barn, to his much reduced flock, in which he noted that it had seemed to him that the whole point of living as the gaunt rabbi suggested long ago meant attentiveness each to each, and shucking gewgaws, and escaping the yoke of possessions, and fleeing the prisons that ritual and tradition can become, and serving each other in person, hand to hand, face to face, and stripping away glitter and acquisitiveness, both personal and communal, and this he had tried to do, with a minimum of bluster, and with full realization of the pain of loss, but he hoped with all his heart that his brothers and sisters would understand and forgive and even perhaps support him in this, for he had tried to live in love, as the gaunt rabbi suggested long ago, a suggestion he thought could, given the chance, given the wholehearted creative relentless support of simple souls like us, change the bone and sinew of the world, and make of this creation a song unlike any that had ever been sung, a world where no child wept in fear, where war was only faint memory, where imagination was food, where no one grappled for power but instead bent every shred of genius to seeing and celebrating the Christ plunged in every soul like a brilliant arrow.

Gone all artsy poetic on us now, the new fella has, said the people in the barn.

On March 19, feast day of Saint Joseph, patron of the dying, the new bishop died, his heart failing utterly as he whipped along the beach road on that green wisp of a bicycle. By pure chance he was found by the young football player who carried the bishop's marrow in his bones. The boy carried the bishop's body to the barn. Two girls later brought the bicycle to the barn also. The bishop's funeral was celebrated by his dear friend the Episcopalian priest, who wore, as instructed by the bishop's last will and testament, his BOSTON COLLEGE POKER TEAM sweatshirt. The bishop's body was then distributed, as also specified by his will, to various organ banks, hospitals, and clinics; one eye ended up in Canada and the other in Oregon, his liver stayed among the islands, and his remaining kidney electrified a carpenter in rural Idaho. What remained after distribution was cremated and scattered in the inlet, as requested by the final codicil in his will. By chance his ashes were flung on an incoming tide, which carried the first serious run of chinook salmon, who in their testy way slashed at everything in or on the water, so a good deal of the bishop ended up in and on the first salmon caught and ceremonially roasted on the beach.

Maybe the new fella was right about it all, after all, said the people, as they sat around the fires that night on the beach, gaping at the stars.

A Note on the Actors

Ben Brimly, playing Major Jones, is delighted to be back with the Weasel Players. More than delighted. Thrilled, moaning, mooing, babbling. There is a spreading stain on his pantaloons.

Elsbeth Moomaw, who first appeared in *The Sun is Our Very Bestest Friend* when she was two years old, has seen her career crater ever since. She is in this production because she is the most supple and pliable and flexible human being the director has ever seen. She can pick a nickel off the floor with her tongue while sitting in a chair. Wouldn't you hire such an actress, and hope for joy beyond your wildest dreams? Well? Thought so.

Edwin Edwards, fresh from the Edinburgh Fringe Festival, where he got lost in the suburbs and ended up working in a chop shop, would like to thank his second wife, Bunni, and his children by his first wife, Krstl, for their support and good cheer during this production. He hopes to someday find a vowel for Krstl.

Betty Furness, of the famous volleyball Furnesses, has been in so many television productions she has lost count. She joins the Weasel Players to get some fecking *theater credit*, which she has fecking well been told fifty fecking *times* that she needs although she sees no particular need for an *extraordinary actress* to have to memorize inane *lines* and perform *night after night* in a tight-fitting *pumpkin* suit when she could fecking well do the usual forty-fecking-second clips before a fecking camera, that's why God invented fecking *cameras*, so people didn't have to endure this sort of prissy fecking *torture* show that they call theat*re*, with a fecking swishy British emphasis on the fecking misspelling of a perfectly good word. The British Empire is *dead*, for feck's sake.

A. Bliss Tokay used to be a horse. She is grateful for major medical insurance.

Plum Tuckered is probably best known for his legendary turn as Ophelia in the Keokuk Players' version of *Rosencrantz and Guildenstern Are Not Actually Dead But in Some Sort of Addled Stupor After Three Days of Watching Ernest Borgnine Movies*, which led to a legal brouhaha. Brouhaha, we observe, is a cool word. Like hullabaloo, isn't that a cool word? Any word that ends with a sprinting parade of vowels or repeated happy phonemes like that is pretty cool. This is why Hawaii is the center of the universe.

Matthew Ridgeway is, *yes*, for chrissake, aware that there was a more *famous* Matthew Ridgeway, it's not like he was never *told* that he is in no way as cool as the famous General Ridgeway, Jesus, how many times can a man be told he is a mere lap poodle compared to his heroic and stern-visaged namesake, who may have saved civilization as we know it, is that a little undue pressure on an artist or what? No wonder he tried to marry his breakfast cereal in Massachusetts.

Elmont C. Phoresus has been.

Sophia Coppola, who is *not* the other Sophia Coppola who won an award for the slowest movie ever made on this sweet earth, my *god*, how a movie that slowly pans over the pitted moonscape of Bill Murray's face for two hours could win an award is beyond me, what kind of stoner epic is *that*, is a six-time Hammy Award winner, which has been worth about eleven cents in her career, she says, snarling like a mink in heat.

Gary Hawthorne Bubble, stage manager for this production, has worked for many years behind the scenes, and has seen goats coupling, a man with a necklace of pigeon feet, a woman wearing cellophane sitting in the orchestra pit (seat 14A, for those of you scoring at home), and an all-children-age-eight production of the Scottish Play, which featured a child saying, no shit, *out, out damned spit*, which made Gary laugh so hard he, no kidding, stained his grunts.

Brian Doyle is the director. He would go at tiresome length into the litany of his tumultuous career in the theater (note spelling, the British Empire is *dead* for heavenssakes) but we just finished rehearsal for the day and Elsbeth Moomaw is my god wearing that pumpkin suit o my god o help me Jesus. There are times when you must forge ahead creatively, or nothing will ever be accomplished, and I would very much like to forge Miss Moomaw creatively. On with the show!

The Subtle Theater

Having been a development officer for the Catholic university for twenty years, Douglas had learned the sign language, the "subtle theater," as he called it, of the donor visit. It began with negotiations by phone: Should he come out to the house? Would they prefer to have lunch on campus? Would they like him to invite Father President also?

As regards this last, the Donnells had declined, being respectful of Father's schedule, "especially during Holy Week," as Mrs Donnell said in her infinitesimally gentle voice. Her voice was so incredibly soft that Douglas could hardly hear her when standing two feet away, let alone on the telephone. Twice he had asked the University's tech service kids to jazz his phone, make it louder, can't we do that? Sir, no, they replied, with their barely hidden grins at his total obtuseness with machinery even as paleozoic as an office phone, with a cord, no less.

But the Donnells, after making various excuses over the past year, had finally relented and allowed him to come to the house, "though not for lunch," as Mr Donnell had said, courtly as ever, eternally the old barrister, "as my lovely bride and I will be fasting during Holy Week, an old family tradition, I am sure it is not by any means universal, and while we would be *delighted*, Douglas, to offer you a light repast, you will surely forgive us for not sharing the meal," to which he had of course replied that if ever there was a man who could stand to miss a meal it was himself, indeed he could stand to miss more than a few, he was sad to say, and it would be refreshing physically and spiritually to share a mere cup of redolent tea, perhaps. It will be rather an ascetic experience, sir, which there are not enough of in today's culture, to be sure.

So on Tuesday he wound through the far western reaches of the city, certain enough of his destination to not refer to the map, but not so certain that he did not stop at a pizza shop to ask for directions. As the scrawny boy at the counter turned to yell into the kitchen, Douglas stared at the gleaming red menu board, but instantly thought better of it; he would reek of cheese, which felt disrespectful, somehow.

The neighborhood in which the Donnells had lived for sixty years, since Mr Donnell returned from the war, had originally been small logging cabins when first settled by "permanent residents," as Mr Donnell phrased it carefully, being a serious scholar of "tribal peoples," as he said, "who were seasonal residents by choice, and we are all in the end tribal peoples, of course, Douglas, we Catholics being a prime example, yes?" But after the enormous firs and cedars were cut, and as the city "metastasized," as Mr Donnell had phrased it, the cabins and cottages gave way to much larger and more ornate houses, and developments by theme, such as Mountain Meadows, in which all the houses looked like ski lodges, and Tuscan View, in which all the houses looked like Italian villas, each one fenced by a row of grapevines. The Donnells' house, originally a logger's cabin, had been renovated beautifully by the developers of Tuscan View, in exchange for four acres of adjacent land, and it too was fenced on three sides by grapevines, although, as Mr Donnell said with a smile, "the grapes were not quite suitable for wine, nor indeed edible by human beings, although they were a source of gustatory delight for the jays and crows every autumn, which pleased Mrs Donnell greatly, my lovely bride being a great fan of the bird tribes, as you know, Douglas."

The first thing Douglas noticed when he approached the house was the shagginess of the fence line; the vines, usually cut as flat as a crewcut, so sharply horizontal that Douglas wondered if the gardeners used a spirit level, were unruly along the sides and nearly chaotic in the back. This was odd, Mr Donnell being a stickler for order in the yard, little as there was of it; he had once explained to Douglas that a clean appearance among the "vegetative tribes," as he called the vines and bushes, was the last vestige of his military habit—"I no longer command men, but I can perhaps persuade the denizens of the yard to be neat in appearance when inspected, Douglas," he said, with his usual half-smile.

Inside the house, though, things seemed shipshape, thought Douglas—fresh flowers in small bowls, floors and windows buffed and shining, a steaming pot of tea on the table. He greeted Mr and Mrs Donnell warmly, made sure to sit as close to Mrs Donnell as possible, and waited for the conversation to open up before bringing up money; another part of the subtle theater of fundraising, he had learned, was patience, and pacing; a visit should have an opening act, an establishment of narrative tone and tenor, before getting down to what amounted to business, and besides, he enjoyed the Donnells' company, their quiet dignity and courtesy, and both of them were gently witty, attentive to wordplay, and quite good storytellers, if you gave them time and space to open up. Mrs Donnell, the daughter of a logger, had been born deep in the fir forests here, and lived for a time in a cottage hollowed from a huge cedar stump, and Mr Donnell, born in Galway, had been an oyster pirate in his youth, among many other adventures.

Now, Douglas, said Mrs Donnell in her preternaturally gentle voice, the mister and I are experimenting with citrus teas of late, so I hope you will not mind having tea made from lemons and oranges, which was delicious, said Douglas, crisp and refreshing, he could feel the vitamins coursing through his bloodstream and cleaning up all the muck and peanut butter lodged there since his boyhood, thank you so much.

They talked about the grapevines; the gardeners are surely terribly busy, said Mr Donnell, what with all the rain lately. They talked about the plunge in housing prices of late, and the startling number of houses for sale in Tuscan View; there are some houses here that have been for sale for two years, said Mrs Donnell quietly, and their owners have gone; we have one friend who now lives in a convent, courtesy of the sisters. They talked about writers and books, the Donnells being ferocious readers, and Douglas noticed that there were far fewer books on the shelves, and the den, formerly crammed with books floor to ceiling, nearly empty; but Mr Donnell explained that he and his lovely bride had suddenly been taken with the urge to purge, as he phrased it, and what with their advancing age they were better off giving the books away to convents and libraries, in the end, than leaving them to be sold in an estate sale, didn't Douglas agree? Of course, said Mrs Donnell with a smile, if the mister and I *had* been graced by children we would happily have inflicted the library on them and *their* children, taking particular care to foist Proust upon the one who never read at all, and Tolstoy upon the one who thought wars were a sensible solution to conflicts, and Robert Louis Stevenson to the one we loved best, and so on in that vein.

After tea Mrs Donnell excused herself to begin preparations for dinner, she said, and Douglas and Mr Donnell walked through the house together, Mr Donnell insisting that Douglas know exactly what the university might expect to eventually own when he and Mrs Donnell returned to the Generosity, as he said. Douglas had been through the house once before, ten years ago, when the university first reestablished contact with the Donnells after a lapse of some years; Douglas, at that time new to the staff, had been assigned the account in the small hope that there might be an annual gift in play, Mr Donnell having had a successful career in the military and Mrs Donnell having inherited a good deal of timberland; privately he also hoped that he might persuade the Donnells eventually to consider an estate gift, which would be rather a feather in his cap.

He had a vague recollection, though, that there had been many more paintings in the house, ten years ago; wasn't Mrs Donnell an avid painter herself, and an astute judge of work from unknown artists, work that had appreciated remarkably over the years? Indeed yes, said Mr Donnell, the house had once been essentially *slathered* in paintings, but in this matter also he and his lovely bride were visited by the urge to purge, and had distributed the works willy nilly, saving only a few of particular emotional value, such as, for example, this lovely little oil of Mrs Donnell's childhood home, now regrettably gone, but not in eternal memory, eh?

At one point Douglas reached for the back door, intending to open it for Mr Donnell so they could step out and glance at the back yard, which Douglas remembered lush with flowers, but Mr Donnell directed him upstairs, to show another of Mrs Donnell's lovely little oils, this one of the logging camp where her father worked, a site "rife with huckleberries in season," noted Mr Donnell, and what is more delicious than huckleberries fresh from the bush? But as Mr Donnell waxed eloquent about those treasures of the high country, as he said, Douglas glanced out the window and noticed that the backyard was completely planted in vegetables: tomatoes, squash, beans, peppers, garlic, and what seemed to be berry bushes; not a single flower remained from the lush garden he remembered.

Nor was there a car, he realized; and the Donnells' glittering black car he remembered very well, for it was, or had been, a meticulously cared-for 1963 Ford Falcon, an absolute jewel of a car, kept in mint condition interestingly not by Mr but by Mrs Donnell, who had learned to fix anything and everything as a child in the woods; now the whole story of the car flooded back upon Douglas—how they had been given the car by her father, how the radio magically played only Christmas music all year long, how you could fill it with gas once a year and miraculously it would survive somehow on that lean diet, how they dearly loved driving it to the beach in summer, the long way, up along the river, which took an extra two hours at least, "but my *heavens*, Douglas, the plethora of birds along the way," Mrs Donnell had said with her eyes alight, "the flotillas of sandhill cranes, the phalanxes of ducks and geese, the mobs and gangs of crows, the osprey and eagles!" And how they would stop to picnic along the river, as Mr Donnell said, "chicken sandwiches and a bottle of wine, and perhaps, if the wind is right and I have lived a good life, a kiss or three from my lovely bride, as a falcon shimmers past; when we speak of heaven, Douglas, that is the heaven I see."

Back downstairs Douglas and Mr Donnell sat for a moment in the den—the lovely wooden table Mr Donnell had brought home from the war was still there, though the books were almost all gone—and went over the papers for the Donnells' estate gift, for which nothing had changed; the university would still get the house and land, and would be responsible for selling whatever possessions remained at the time of their deaths. As for our annual gift, Douglas, said Mr Donnell, my lovely bride and I had discussed elevating it a bit, but we think it would be best for the moment to leave it at a thousand dollars a year, for reasons I am sure you understand. Douglas agreed wholeheartedly and he stood to leave.

Now, Douglas, wait here for a moment and let me go find the small gift Mrs Donnell has prepared for you, said Mr Donnell, and he disappeared down the hallway to the bedroom—a hallway also denuded of paintings, Douglas noticed; he could see the slightly brighter squares where they had hung on the wall. He smiled, though, suddenly remembering the Donnells' customary parting gifts—bottles of superb wine from their remarkable cellar, bottles famous among anyone at the university who had ever had the slightest dealings with the Donnells, who loved fine wines, had a cellar filled with terrific bottles from around the world, and were the rare connoisseurs who liked to give terrific wines away. Douglas, in fact, still had the bottle from his visit ten years before, a bottle so legendary that he was loathe to open it, and was saving it to drink with his wife and son when their third and last child graduated from college.

Now then, Douglas, said Mr Donnell, returning from the dim hallway, and he opened his hands to reveal a glorious tomato. That is as fresh and succulent a gift as you will be given today, I'd warrant, said Mr Donnell, smiling. The tomato, you remember, is actually a berry. If we were truly generous we would be handing you a hatful of huckleberries, but we have not as yet gone a-berrying, as my lovely bride likes to say. Now, Douglas, Mrs Donnell is down for her afternoon nap, so she has asked me to say farewell for her, which I cannot do with her exquisite eloquence, so I will simply say farewell, and express our most sincere thanks for the kindness of your visit. I hope you know how very much we savor the university's crucial work, and we are delighted to be able to support it in even such a small way as we do. But perhaps the house and yard, when they come into your possession, will go some small way toward making the wonderful education there possible for a boy or girl who would otherwise struggle to make ends meet.

They shook hands at the door, and Douglas looked around the living room one last time, knowing he would not be back again until the day he stood in this exact spot with the estate assessor; and now he saw as if with new eyes; indeed the floors were brilliant and shining, because the rugs that had lain upon them were gone; and the bright cloths that covered the arms of the couch had been cut from old towels; and the pair of work-boots behind the door had been patched so many times that the patches had patches; and the grapevines he could see through the window were riotous because Mr Donnell had probably canceled the gardening service, which he could no longer afford, and at his age could not climb the ladder to trim them himself, as he had meticulously trimmed everything else he could reach in the yard; and the books had been sold for money to live on, and the paintings had been sold for money to live on, and the cellar of superb wines had been sold for money to live on, and the flowers were gone because they could not be eaten, and the absolute jewel of a car had been sold, probably with copious tears, for money to live on, and Douglas would bet everything he owned that no lunch had been served today not because they were fasting for Holy Week but because there was no lunch to serve, and no actual tea had been served because there was no tea, and that dinner for them tonight would be a few vegetables from the garden, and God alone knew how the Donnells found the thousand dollars a year for their annual gift to the university, and their quiet plan was to hold on to their lives and dignity and privacy by a thread until they died, and they would die smiling, having held to their own form of quiet grace until the very end of their lives, in which each thought that the love of the other was the greatest gift imaginable.

He drove to the university in silence. Back in his office he thought for a while and then wrote the Donnells a letter of thanks for the visit in which he confirmed the agreement as regards the house and land as estate gift upon decease, but also noted with a sigh that he had himself made a bookkeeping mistake, God save us all from such fools as I, and that their annual gift of a thousand dollars had already been credited for this year, he had just discovered, so he was returning a thousand dollars with his apologies and thanks, as per the university's strict regulations, which specified that annual gifts could not be banked in advance of the year of their application. He printed out the letter and signed it and folded it and then unfolded it and wrote, in the awful cramped handwriting he had been ashamed of since he was a small boy, *I hope you know how much I admire you both, and thank you for your extraordinary generosity to me and to the university. To know you has been not only a gift but a lesson in what it really means when we talk about grace and courage. Your good friend, Douglas.*

On Flinging the Dog

*So to bed, where my wife and I had some high words upon my telling
her that I would fling the dog which her brother had gave her out the
window if he pissed the house any more.*

—Samuel Pepys, February 12, 1660

The first thing you want to ask, upon reading this snippet of Mr
P's famous daily confession, is why not title this essay "On Pissing
the House," which is a very good question, an *excellent* question,
thank you.

Moving along, why does Pepys use a comma, right off the bat,
where he doesn't really need one, and then he just lays the whole
idea, of using commas, down to die, after that? And the whole
which her brother had gave her, doesn't that sound like Bill Clin-
ton on his fifth cheeseburger? You can just see old Bill late at night
with a whiskey in each hand happily regaling a weary state trooper
about a dog which a mistress had give him who pissed the house,
and the poor trooper, let's call him Lester, he's thinking was it the
dog or the mistress pissed the house? Because he has heard stories
down in the barracks will make you pass a weasel laughing. But ol'
Bill is off and running now about the marijuana he did not *no* sir *no*
way *in*hale despite having it burning redolently under his capacious
nose which despite what *sum*bitch who weren't even *there* be flinging insinuations to the rap*scal*lions of the media, Lester, the cold
hard left *nut* of the matter is that *no* one was there at that point in
time, including me in a manner of speaking, you know your meta-
physics, Lester, I assume you do and not even the fella whose room

it was which I don't know who he was neither, was there, so there y'are, pass me that bottle there.

Then there is the phrase *my wife and I had high words*, which we have all had, with our spouse of whatever gender or degree of gender he or she or whatever is at, now during *my* presidency, Lester, you didn't see the gummint of the U Nited States sticking its pepys into the business of people searching diligently for their gender iden*ty*, be they even from *Georgia* or whatsowherever, during *my* presidency we had bigger frogs to fry, which namely was world peace and pros*per*ty, but *some* administration's tit got caught in the wringer of *some* first lady's starvin' for *health* care reform, which *those* three words'll make you piss the house and that's a fact. Go on, Lester, say 'em aloud and see if your bladder don't go all Tip O'Neill on you, son. And then you *really* want to piss the house, ponder *some* former first lady we know almost actually swearin' in as *POTUS*, which I don't want to have to tell you would mean lot of people sayin' *health care reform* which words you don't want to say without you have a towel ready to hand, I tell you *that*. Don't spit whiskey out your nose like that, Lester, it's indecent.

Finally let us consider the flinging of the dog, or prospective flinging of the dog, which occasioned the high words, and which was itself occasioned by the pissing of the house. Myself, now, Lester, I have flang a dog or two in my time, there are times when the dog must be flang, and you got to get your legs under you for that, it's done with the haunches, like pitchin' and politickin', you get a good grip on the scruff of her neck, now, and you crouch down real low, and one real smooth real quick motion and out she goes, Lester, caterwaulin' like a wolf what's gay and *proud* of it, her old mauve pant suit flappin' like a flag, and those three awful words all shreddin' in the wind, heeeeeaaallthhhhhhh caaaaaaaaaaaare reeeeeeform, *don't* shoot whiskey out your nose, Lester, people'll think you're from Georgia for heavenssake, all due respect to the Pee Pit State.

A Note on Countification

It began, as many brilliant and complex things begin, in a pub. The owner was a man named Dennis, a widely liked and respected soul. Like many men, he was nostalgic for a past that had never existed, but yearning for something that never was is an ancient human characteristic and vice, and certainly it has in many cases been turned to lovely use; in film and song for example.

It is song where this story begins. Dennis had a lovely baritone and often would close the evening in his pub by singing songs of the west of Ireland. Soon he was joined in song by other men whose families traced back to the west of Ireland. In time two of those men, along with Dennis, the three who traced their families back to Galway, established the custom that seating in the pub would be by family ancestry: men and women whose families traced back to the counties of the west of Ireland sat on the west side of the pub, those from the east the east, and so on. People whose families traced back to other nations were assigned seats depending on their ancestral countries' geographical relationship to Ireland—Scottish people to the north, Hungarians to the east, Koreans to the west, and so on.

Soon Dennis's pub grew famous for this seating arrangement, which he dubbed, memorably, countification. Journalists, especially television people, could not resist the colorful and often funny stories of seating decisions made on the fly, usually by Dennis—in this way people of Inuit ancestry were assigned to County Antrim, and Chileans were considered the children of Cork—and the entertaining stories that ensued of friendships born and even marriages made, the most famous such marriage being the Romanian girl who married a boy whose family traced their ancestry to County Kildare, the wedding reception held at the pub.

Soon Dennis was renowned enough to be asked to stand for public office, first locally, as candidate for the City Council, and then statewide, as candidate for the state senate. He won both of these seats, and in both positions advocated the idea, at first entertaining but then increasingly popular, of rearranging the city and then the state along ancestral lines. What began as a funny story—Dennis and several of his friends from the pub moving to various parts of the city according to which region of Ireland their ancestors were from, much reported on television and then by a series of national media outlets—soon became a movement, variously described as refreshingly respectful of ancestral identity, reverential and celebratory of familial nationality, or bigoted and fascist to a scurrilous and possibly criminal and unconstitutional degree. To everyone's surprise, people of every conceivable ancestral nationality picked up stakes and moved as fast and lightly as they could; people left behind possessions and even houses in their haste to move to the section of the city, and later the state, where people of their ancestral legacy had settled.

This gave rise to a raft of problems. People who had lived their whole lives in the city found themselves now living in the remote sage desert of the southeastern corner of the state, for example, because that is where people from Counties Wexford and Carlow had settled, not to mention southeastern European countries and the south Pacific islands, including Australia. And what to make of mixed marriages, and people who had lost the thread of their ancestral legacies, and people of, say, eight different ancestral nationalities? Could you choose one ancestral legacy over another? Could you trade with someone else? If you lied about your ancestral legacy, and were caught in the lie, should you be arrested, or fined, or repatriated to another legacy's settlement? And what records were to be considered legitimate proof of legacy? Were treasured family stories legal tender? Old photographs? What about people whose ancestors were from countries that do not exist anymore? What about people whose ancestors were forcibly ejected from their original countries? Could they claim the legacy of the original country, despite historical turmoil, or did they have to assume the ancestral legacy of the country their ancestors had been sent, or exiled, to?

To deal with these questions, civil adjudication courts were created, but this effort too soon became embroiled in all sorts of further questions. Which courts had authority over which questions? If a man of Albanian ancestry sold his house in the north side of the city, so as to buy a house on the east side of the city, where those of Albanian ancestry lived cheek by jowl with people from Wicklow and Dublin, and the price of his first house had plummeted by virtue of public knowledge of impending sales by people of his ancestry, and the price of the second house had risen to shocking heights because of the reverse, was he entitled to any public redress or relief? Could he sue Dennis for setting this market aberration in motion? Is any one individual responsible for fluctuations in the market?

Despite the welter of legal and economic problems set in motion by Dennis's idea, he remained personally remarkably popular with the electorate, and was soon elected governor by a wide margin, a vote of confidence he interpreted as a mandate to speak openly of the death of the melting pot, the primacy of ancestry, and the virtues of ethnic separation, and soon he was being mentioned as a national candidate for office on a platform of respect for the past, reverence for ancestors, creative management of real estate markets and a new series of investment funds created to influence and adjust that market, and the renaissance of public song at any and all civic and civil events. Even before his successful third-party candidacy for president, the national real estate market achieved a historic frenzy, as people of Asian legacy moved to the west and southwest, people of European ancestry moved to the east and northeast, people of Hispanic and Indian ancestry populated the south, and vast stretches of the north were set aside for people of no known, or disputed, ancestry, in reservations popularly called the Blanklands. People whose ancestors had been members of the original 500 nations of North America before the continent's "discovery" moved to the center of the country, a tremendous swatch of land comprising what had been Nebraska, Iowa, Kansas, and Missouri.

A number of positive results of this sea change in American life were trumpeted by Dennis and his colleagues (many of them his original companions in the pub) in subsequent electoral debates and public forums. The energy of the real estate market resurrected a national economy that had been fallow for years. The reorganization of political arrangements and capital fomented the rise of new parties of sometimes startling character—the Welsh Estonian Uruguayan Alliance, for example. The public cost of racism and its redress declined by virtue of the essentially normalized aspect of race and ethnicity; it appears likely that the political parties vying for power in the next election will be called simply White, Brown, Black, Red, and Green. Public education, what with the sharp rise in legacy and ancestral studies in colleges, foundations, and entrepreneurial ventures, is better funded than at any time in recent memory. The beneficial effect on the arts is evident; the warming trend in international relations among countries avid for the economic and political benefit of close arrangements with their American "cousins," as the popular term has it, is documented; and even problems like the lack of housing for people of Monte Carlan descent are admittedly less pressing than some of the social and civic ills to which this nation, in all too clear recent memory, was subjected. It maybe be too bold to say, as Dennis has said many times in many venues, that the movement sometimes called Proud Separation has saved us from national collapse and oblivion, and there remain some observers who object, in some cases stridently and vociferously, that institutionalized racism has not solved problems but created bigger and more intractable ones that will lead eventually to walls and wars; but there are detractors to every great idea and enterprise, as Dennis says, and it may well be the case, he often adds in his speeches, that if history tells us true, the more detractors there are, the better the idea; a remark he has made more than once as he has advanced the idea of countification writ large. Planetary countification is an idea whose time has come, he says, with his usual cheerful simplicity, and song at the end of his appearance; and imagine the future, in which countification is the settlement principle among the worlds we will reach in the centuries to come. The planet Galway, the planet Burma—would those be such bad ideas, in the end?

KXMS

The radio station KXMS opened in 1956, late in the summer, as a station playing only Christmas music, and for a long time it was curiously successful, with a high point of some half a million listeners in the greater metropolitan area and a waiting list for advertisers; but eventually its fortunes declined, as the culture generally became more secular and less religious, and by the turn of the century the station had fallen upon hard times. There was a brief surge of popularity again in the months after the murders of September 11, for reasons that would be interesting to speculate about, but by 2012 the station's parent corporation was actively looking to sell or close the business, most of the air time was pre-recorded and unadorned by live comment, and the staff had been reduced to three, two of whom recruited advertising revenue with all their might.

The third staffer was a man named Thomas Murphy, age fifty. Thomas was the talent, so to speak, still hosting the station's one live show, a late-night stint featuring unusual Christmas music (jazz and reggae versions of standards, for example) and the occasional specials on holiday and religious music of other cultures and traditions; his specials on Mormon holidays were especially popular, particularly the April 6 show, celebrating Jesus' birthday in Latter-day Saints tradition, and May 15, the day that John the Baptist is said to have appeared to Joseph Smith in upstate New York.

But Thomas was no fool; he saw the future, and the future did not include disk jockeys making enough money to send their twin daughters to college. For a while he milked his contacts in radio and television diligently for job leads, but everyone he knew professionally was in the same boat, and equally desperate for new jobs; he considered teaching at a community college or a high school, but education budgets were in free fall; he pondered quitting to write novels or screenplays, but as his wry wife Eileen remarked, quitting a job to be an artist was tantamount to giving up money altogether, which doesn't seem like a particularly wise decision at this particular juncture, does it, Thomas?

As September turned to October and Thomas scrambled to pay the girls' school fees, he found himself trimming his personal budget; no longer did he treat himself to lunch here and there, no longer did he buy beers occasionally for his friends after work, no longer did he buy books or music; that's why God invented libraries, as he said.

So that one bright fall morning when Thomas approached the station, and found the front door blocked by a grim Girl Scout, in full regalia, he thought for a surreal instant that the station had finally gone out of business, and defense against looters had been subcontracted out to the Girl Scouts, before he noticed a mountain of cookie boxes on a table.

Would you like the buy some Girl Scout cookies? said the child, grimly.

Love to, said Thomas, but I bought several boxes yesterday at the library.

This was a roaring lie; in fact he had lied to the Scout at the library about buying cookies at the grocery store, and now dreaded the lie he would have to tell at the grocery when she asked him to buy cookies. There were days when he thought the Girl Scouts were tiny racketeers.

Several boxes? said the Girl Scout, sternly. How many is several?

Ah . . . five, said Thomas.

What kind?

Pardon me?

What kind of cookies did you buy?

Thin Mints. Five boxes.

Liar.

I beg your pardon?

That's a lie. We are not selling Thin Mints yet. We don't sell Thin Mints for another week. We start out with the other kinds and then close hard with the Thin Mints. It's like the Feast of Cana—we finish with the best.

Cana?

The Feast of Cana. Where the guy made wine from water.

Right, said Thomas. Well, I must go.

You owe me fifteen dollars.

What?

You said you bought five boxes, but that's a lie. You know it and I know it. You might as well just face up to it and fork over the cash. We take checks also. No cards.

Right here, thought Thomas later, he could have simply walked away smiling, but some odd fictive impulse in him awoke, and he leaned over the table and looked down at the girl—MARGRET, said her name tag—and said, in his most reasonable sonorous velvety radio voice, well, *Margret*, I actually *did* buy five boxes of Thin Mints yesterday, at the library, and I happen to know the girl who sold them to me quite well, because she's my *daughter*.

He smiled, to ameliorate the sting of checkmate, and then turned to enter the station when he heard her voice behind him:

What's her troop?

He said the first number that entered his head, knowing that brisk confidence was his only hope: 23.

Liar. There is no Troop 23.

Yes, there is.

No, there isn't. That's the second lie you have told me in three minutes.

Thomas fled into the station and stayed slightly rattled all the way up the stairs and down the echoing empty line of offices until he reached his own. Here he calmed down, feeling at home—he had been in this office for twenty years, and had turned it into something of a warm den, filled with mementos and a tape library of his best shows. I really should have that digitized before the station closes altogether, he thought, not for the first time; but as usual he forgot about what he should do as soon as he started into what he did, which was become completely absorbed in music and obscure recordings and interviews with remarkable musicians and musical scholars, and plot out four-hour adventures in, say, music in Aramaic, or a whole show devoted to music about the Madonna, or a show honoring each of the animals present in the stable that miraculous day (you would be surprised how very many songs there are about sheep). Thomas was one of those rare and lucky souls who was very good indeed at the one thing he loved to do; as his wry wife had often observed, he very probably would continue to do the thing he loved to do even when it ceased to provide a living for the family, which is part of the reason she had become a teacher ten years before; she knew him well, and saw the future better than he did, but loved him thoroughly, and thought she would do her best to protect his joy when the crash came.

At lunchtime, as usual now, he had an apple, chewing slowly so as to savor each slice and pretend that it was a larger lunch than it was.

During the afternoon he made phone calls for the two advertising men; in rare cases the fact that Thomas himself, the talent, was on the phone with a potential customer sealed the deal, and it was Thomas who had suggested that they branch out and begin to call and apply for cultural grants, and look into possible benefactors who also might be slightly impressed that Thomas himself was on the phone, or in their offices, beaming.

He left at five, having completely forgotten about the grim Girl Scout, but to his surprise there she was at her cookie table, glaring at him.

Bring the money tomorrow, she said, with the same grim tone she had used before.

Listen, kid, I don't really want your cookies, and I have to tell you there's only three of us left in our offices, so it's not like you are going to break the bank here, okay?

I sold more than a hundred boxes today, she said. Tomorrow I'll sell a hundred and fifty. Not counting your five boxes.

He gaped; a hundred boxes?

I'll be here all week, she said, and my goal is a thousand boxes.

He stood there transfixed. By the end of the week this child would make more money than he made, by far. And for the Girl Scouts! The green mafia!

I'll make you a deal, kid, he said. I'll bring your money tomorrow. In fact I'll buy ten boxes. In exchange for which you come to a staff meeting. Bring your mother or your manager or whomever is in charge of your protection ring. See you in the morning.

In this odd fashion began the renaissance of KXMS, its resurrection, as it were, from the bottom of the ratings and advertising pool to today's renown; Thomas later found it difficult to explain exactly what he saw in Margret that led to the meeting, but he much enjoyed telling the story of the meeting, and how within a few minutes he and the advertising men were gaping as Margret laid out plans for advertising incursion into the Jewish community ("There would be no Christmas without Rabbi Jesus"), the Muslim community ("All prophets are honored at Christmas"), the vast and intricate Protestant community ("Christmas is the one time a year when all Christians are home under the same roof"), and even, as she said, the uniformed community; the advertising men for a moment thought she meant the armed forces, but Margret had bigger plans; every Brownie, Girl Scout, Boy Scout, Cub Scout, Sea Scout, and Campfire Girl in the tri-state area would, in her vision, soon be an agent and ambassador—essentially a small advertising executive—for KXMS, appealing to not only their parents but to their entire family circle; a plan that reaped spectacular results among the Mormon and Hispanic communities, with their large numbers of children, and concomitantly, aunts and cousins, etc.

By the summer of 2013 the station was not only in the black but earning so much in advertising revenue that corporate took it off the market; by Christmas 2013, the station had quadrupled its listenership, and, under Margret's direction, established a serious online presence; by summer 2014 the station had been the subject of, at last count, more than a hundred adulatory stories in print and electronic media around the world; and in the fall of 2014, as Thomas and his wry wife drove the twins to college, Thomas could revel in what one major newspaper had called one of the most amazing and brilliant media turnarounds in modern business history. And well he might have reveled, too, as a man who had worked hard and well in his chosen profession; except that, as they drove up a lovely alley of immense elm trees, his wry wife remarked that eventually Margret would have to go to college also. Thomas's heart sank for a moment; but then he calculated that Margret had four more years running the station before she matriculated, and by then he could, with a good conscience, retire. As they parked and unloaded the car, he insisted that each of them eat a Thin Mint, for luck, and then they made their way to the residence halls, Thomas humming Christmas songs.

When You're Out of Schlitz, You're Out of Beer

The elementary school Christmas musical production season being upon us again like a cougar on a fawn, I am powerfully reminded of my own first experience in musical theater, the memory of which still makes my mother spit her apple tea across the table when I bring up such things as a Hickory Tree peeing in his pants, and a Striped Bass assaulting an Eggplant, and, my mom's favorite moment, a young teacher cursing in Gaelic into her microphone near the end, and my dad's favorite moment, my kid brother Tommy suddenly singing *when you're out of Schlitz, you're out of beer,* which was not in the script at all, and was something of a conundrum, as my dad says in his inimitable style, as the boy did not drink beer, no one in the house drank beer, and if any of us *were* to drink beer, certainly we would not be drinking such a vulgar amalgam of wet air and insipid jingles, purveyed in cans of suspicious origin, which is how my dad talks.

This musical production was in the auditorium of Saint John Vianney Grade School, near the Atlantic Ocean, which is how we came to have a Striped Bass in the Production, as the young teacher was a student of Local Flora and Fauna, and allowed her charges, the fifth grade plus a few slumming kindergartners (thus my kid brother Tommy) to choose any local plant or animal to impersonate, although she overruled a few choices, like rumrunners and gunsels. My memory is not what it used to be, but I have a clear memory of a ragged front line of Ducks and Potatoes, those being

then the most famous products of our island, and then a taller motley back line of Fish, Bushes, Trees, Birds, Deer, and a Horseshoe
Crab, this being a boy whose mother worked in the theater. My kid
brother Tommy was a Horse, which suited him, for you never saw a
child who looked more like a Horse, it was a stone miracle how that
boy managed to carry his huge head around as a child, and I was an
Apple, because my mother had burned all her time on my brother
Tommy, who was weeping because he couldn't get his Horse cos-
tume over his incredible head, and my mom had abandoned me to
my sister, who stuffed me into a red jacket and told me I was now
an Apple, and if I complained to mom she would snap my fingers
like twigs.

I remember that there was a Flounder near me, a silent boy
named Michael, and an Osprey, a foul-tempered girl named Grace,
and my friend Billy, the tallest boy in the class, who was a Glossy
Ibis, and I remember my mom and dad and brothers and sisters sitting near the statue of Saint John Vianney the Confessor, my sister
ostentatiously glaring and cracking her knuckles, and that's all I remember of the Production, other than the ripple as people moved
away from the sobbing Hickory Tree. My dad, however, is one of
those rare souls whose memory has improved remarkably as he has
aged, and he says he remembers the day as golden and miraculous
as if it were born yesterday.

You were so terrified we thought you would faint, he says, and
your friend Billy, the tall boy, looked queasy beyond compare, but
your brother Tommy looked calm and cheerful, probably because
no child ever looked more like the part he was to play. Your mother
does not like to speak of this, but that boy had a head like a suitcase.
He had the single largest head I have ever seen on a human being,
big enough to require its own zip code. His head was so big it had
different *weather* on either side. Try to imagine what it was like
bringing this child to the barber. Try to imagine the expenditure.
Anyway the Production started well but quickly fell apart, and indeed the young teacher, who was from a large family in Scotland,
as I recall, used foul and vulgar language in the old tongue. Things
fell apart further and then for murky reasons your brother Tommy

stepped forward suddenly and sang that beer jingle, a moment I will savor on my deathbed.

Some moments, continues my dad, are unforgettable for reasons we cannot articulate, and for me that is certainly one of them. It is not every afternoon, I think I can safely say, that a boy with a head the size of a suitcase sings a beer jingle on stage in an auditorium featuring not one but four statues of the Madonna in various stages of Her holy and blameless life. Other than the moments during which you children were born, and the moment your mother married me, and the moment she did not die on the surgeon's table, and the moment the war ended and I was not dead as she and I expected me to be, I believe that might be the greatest moment of my life. You and your brothers and sister and mother were all there, Gaelic was in the air, the Madonna hovered nearby with Her enigmatic smile, we were all young and strong and in the fullness of our days, and humor, which is the greatest and holiest of gifts and virtues, as you know, was everywhere like a generous ocean. Your mother does not remember that day as clearly as I do, but *I* remember it as if it emerged a moment ago from the unimaginable hand of the Maker, and that was a holy day. *When you're out of Schlitz, you're out of beer*, sweet Jesus, where that boy learned that is a mystery to me. I think I better lie down now, but not before I become as the Hickory Tree, profligate with the waters of the Lord released upon the dry and thirsty earth.

It's All About Teeth, in the End

And while I am on the subject of elementary school holiday music productions, which I feel should be regulated like any other controlled substance, I am reminded of the Easter pageant, again at Saint John Vianney School near the Atlantic Ocean, when *another* one of my brothers, not the one who suddenly stepped forward during the Christmas musical and sang *when you're out of Schlitz, you're out of beer*, which still sends my father into a happy coma when he remembers it, emerged from an enormous cardboard Easter egg on the stage and said in a voice that shook the rafters, *Jesus Fucking Christ, it's hot in there*, which caused our father to laugh so hard he sprained an eyeball, he said. Bless my hoary soul, says my dad when I reminded him of this last night, do not under any circumstances remind your mother of that, or she will spit her tea on me, which she does on a regular basis when caught by surprise, which I think indicates a problem with her dentures. If we do not pay close attention to dental engineering, I feel, the terrorists will have won, which is a good example of the way my dad talks, sailing smoothly from the earth into an asteroid field without turn signals, and often laughing so hard at his own narrative that he loses his spleen and has to search under the couch cushions for it, as he tells his granddaughters, who gaze at him in amazement like children gaping at the endless stars.

My dad says the Easter pageant slid into a dullness so thorough after Peter's remark that he fell asleep and drooled on himself such that a pool formed and the National Guard came, but my mother, by now on the extension phone, says this is a roaring lie, it was the *Coast* Guard, which sets the two of them to laughing so hard my mom said she had to lie down or there would be an accident and hell to pay, so my dad commandeered the conversation and said he could remember at least ten mortifying and hilarious events for each of the children, which is a total of eighty incredible moments, if you do the math, which was never exactly your strong suit, my boy, which reminds me of a story. This is how my dad talks, like a driver who is parading along only slightly over the speed limit and suddenly he sees a cat that he can get an angle on if he guns the engine. It was hard enough for you to get the concept of paired *body* parts down when you were a lad, says my dad, you were always losing track of how many feet and hands you had but also losing shoes and gloves at a terrific rate, not to mention the time when you started losing your pants also, it was unnerving for everyone concerned to see you come trotting around the corner from kindergarten wearing only your eyeglasses. But my point is that while you finally *did* grasp the concept of two hands and feet and ears and eyes, probably during college, I vividly remember the one time your brother Kevin the math genius sat down to help you with your homework and he grew so frustrated that he *chewed and swallowed his own teeth*, which is why he also wears dentures today. It's all about teeth in the end, as Saint Luke says in the gospels.

This is how my dad talks, which is why his appearances as a lector at Mass, for example, draw such crowds, but my brothers and I think that he is more on his game at home, where he does not have to wear a suit and tie, and can wander around in the slippers he has had since he served with Lincoln in the Revolutionary War, as he says, waving his cigar like a wand, and talking about the time our sister spent a week trying to teach a kitten to speak. I admired the child's open heart, says my dad, but after a week I had to take her aside, when your mother was out of the house, and point out that cats, even tiny ones, are the spawn of Satan, and many years ago Saint Matthew forbade them to speak. Yet cats, as I informed your sister, do have one use in this world; they are why God invented cars, as it says somewhere in the Gospel of John.

The Guest Speaker

At the end of May, ten days before school ended, the teacher welcomed a surprise guest to class. The syllabus was the oral and written history of the Vietnam war. This was the last day the class would spend in Vietnam; on Monday they would begin a week's discussion of Grenada, Panama, Bosnia, Somalia, Afghanistan, and Iraq, with a brief discussion of the role of American troops as part of United Nations forces, American troops as covert operators in zones of influence, and American non-military forces in action worldwide as spies, bribemasters, jailers, torturers, shippers of weapons, negotiators, and merchants of products and services never seen or reported upon by the general public except in times of accidental revelation, revolution, or reorganization. To finish the year they would spend a week on American troops as agents of liberty, necessary bullies, advocates of the hideously oppressed, defenders of the hunted and helpless and speechless, avengers of the wronged, and cheerfully grim stalwart leaders of alliances against dictators, murderers, madmen, warlords, gangsters, and holy criminals of every ostensible spiritual persuasion.

But today, having finished the formal syllabus, the teacher announces a guest, and Dave and Moon and everyone else relax and slouch and sprawl in their chairs, for The Guest Speaker is an ancient and awful tradition, it's always some ostensible expert or authority or scholar or pompous ass who lectures and homilizes and sermonizes and drones and blathers, and you need not pay the slightest attention unless there is extra credit, which there is not, so all you need to do to survive The Guest Speaker is put on a mask of slight interest, lean back comfortably, try not to nod off, try not to drool on yourself, and dream of girls or summer or cars or how delicious it would be to put your head down on your syllabus and nap for the next hour.

But then The Guest Speaker walks in and Dave and Moon sit up straight, astonished, for it is, no kidding, amazingly, against all sense and reason, unbelievably, inarguably, Dave's dad.

Dave is immediately mortified. Who knows what the old man will burble on about this time? Dave has heard his dad expound on a hundred subjects, none of them riveting and all of them boring beyond belief: dendrology, silvology, ichthyology, the nature of forbs and sedges and rushes and the difference among them as regards reproductive gear, ungulates and their development as a species west of the Cascades, saws and axes and the history of log rafts on the Columbia River and its tributaries, the advent of the donkey-engine in the forests of Oregon and its impact culturally and economically, the history of libraries in America with particular attention to Andrew Carnegie and his ideas about access and circulation, the genius of bookmobiles, the few but admirable cases of book-boats, the custom of universal military drafts and compulsory service with particular attention paid to comparative practice in the countries of the West, the natural history of the Zigzag River from its source in the glacier to its conjunction with the Sandy River with sidelong commentary on how rivers, even rivers as brief as the Zigzag constantly reshape and reinvent themselves so that you cannot in good conscience say with any accuracy or pretense toward truth or fact that the Zigzag for example is the same river today as it was yesterday, and how everyone says, well, that's because the water in it is never the same minute to minute, but far more interesting is that the shape and size and breadth and volume and direction and progress of the river is never the same because it is always slicing away at its boundaries and being incurred upon by collapsing banks and being partially dammed by the collapse of trees and rockslides, isn't that so, Dave?

But this is not what his dad talks about today. His dad sits quietly on a stool at the front of class, not looking at Dave, and the teacher asks him questions for a few minutes about his service in the war. Branch of service? Length of tour? Equipment? Training? Pay? Benefits? Location in country? Transportation to and from war?

Dave is still sitting up straight. He had heard none of this. His dad does not talk about the war. It is unspeakable and so I will not speak of it, he says. All Dave knows is that his dad will not touch a gun nor allow a gun in their house or on their property, what little property they have. One time an uncle came to visit and in his car he had a shotgun with which he was going to hunt quail and Dave's dad made him park the car out by the highway and walk into the cabin so that the gun would not be on their property, what little there was of it.

But here is Dave's dad talking about rifles and machine guns. Here he is talking about trip wires and sharpened wooden stakes. Here he is talking about a roasted baby he saw smoldering in a bomb crater. Here he is talking about a girl who had been raped so many times she never walked again. Here he is talking about a man he knew who collected the ears and tongues and penises of dead men. Here he is talking about a man he knew who lost his mind and control of his bowels during a single night and never regained either of those functions. Here he is talking about a man who was the only man to survive an attack and he was so covered with the blood and brain material of his best friends that he stripped off all his clothes and equipment and ran into the jungle screaming. Here he is talking about a boy he knew who had said he was eighteen but it turned out he was fifteen, almost sixteen, and he survived until the last week of their tour and with six days to go before he escaped, he dove into a river and hit a mine and all that was left of him was a thumb and a kneecap. Here he is looking directly at Dave and saying war is ancient. War is us. We have always been at war. When will we stop? Perhaps you can dream a way to stop. I cannot see that but perhaps you can. You are the age we were when we went to that country and never came back. Who we were then never came back. Some of our bodies came back but not who we were before. You can maybe dream a way to make that stop. To solve an argument by shooting someone in the belly or the face is not a good way to solve an argument. His friends will shoot you, and then your friends will shoot them, and on and on it goes. Perhaps you can dream a way to make it stop. I will tell you a story. One day I couldn't take it anymore. I went to my commander and told him. He said okay fine then you are on field duty. Field duty is when you go pick up pieces of men and boys after a battle. You want to separate all your pieces from the other side's pieces. You have to match the pieces as best you can. This head with this torso, this leg with its matching leg, this foot with this leg. Hands are the hardest. I am sure I often put the wrong hand with the wrong arm. I did the best I could. Our hands were just as brown and dirty as their hands. Some of their heads belonged to boys your age, Dave. You too, Moon. I did the best I could. When you gathered all the pieces and put them into little piles, other men would come and bag the piles and affix name tags if we were sure who was who. I am sure there were some pieces in the wrong bags but who knows? Sometimes there were extra pieces still in the field after the bags were evacuated. How could that be? I don't know. Yet there would be a hand or a foot. Sometimes you would find just one small part that didn't look like anything you ever knew before but you got to recognize those things, like elbows and kneecaps and shoulder blades. I would bury all the extra parts and tamp down the dirt tenderly and then urinate on the dirt to keep animals away. I would mark the territory. I did these things. That is what I did. I never spoke about those things before. Not even to my own son whom I love more than any other young man in the world. Not even to him. I couldn't bring myself to have those things in my mouth any more. If I could ask any one favor of you it is that you remember what I did. If I could ask another favor it is that you dream a way to make those things impossible. The greatest weapon ever invented is your imagination. You could study history the rest of your life and it's all solving arguments by shooting people in the belly or cutting their heads off or raping their daughters or roasting their infants. We can do better than that. We are the animals of wild imagination.

We can make our dreams come true right here in this world, right now, right this minute. We can imagine a new history. If I could ask you a third favor it is that you actually listen to what I am saying. I know who you are behind your masks and disguises. I know every one of you. I have known many of you since you were infants. I see you behind your faces and I ask that you remember what I am saying. Not for the horror but for the possibility. I'll never not be in that field. I'll be in that field the rest of my life. But you don't have to be, and your children, and your children's children. Dream me a way to walk out of that field. This I beg of you. Thank you.

And he rose from the stool, in the shivering silence, and moved toward the door; but up rose his son, and he ran to his father, he ran, I tell you, he *ran* down the aisle between the fourth and fifth rows, and embraced his father, and the son wept, and the father wept, and there were many there that day who wept also, and wept again later in the telling of this, and many the listener wept also in the hearing of this, before that day was done.

Sachiel the Tailor

Another time I was talking to Sachiel, the tailor in Boston whose shop on Chauncy Street was essentially a door with a vast and impenetrable space behind it, a wilderness known only to Sachiel, who never moved from his stool by the door during working hours, and we got to talking all metaphysical, as he said, about his work.

Now, what you see of my work is tactile, he said—pants, jackets, buttons, zippers, the occasional nice shirt, although not in your case, your shirts are a despair to me and very probably to your poor mother, if only she knew. Whereas what I sometimes think my work is, is holes, do you know what I am saying? A young man like you comes to me because a seam has burst in his jacket, and well it should burst, such shoddy workmanship I have not seen since I was a boy in the ancient and long ago. I repair the hole—I *vanish* the hole, you see? So my work is vanishing holes. Holes present themselves, like that hole in the breast pocket of this awful shirt you are for some reason wearing today, what is that, Egyptian cotton? Why does someone wear such a thing? Maybe such a thing is good for a man working in the cotton fields near Alexandria but in Boston I don't think so. What I am saying is that holes come and I make them go. I am in the business of closing holes. If all was well, if all things *kept* their composition, then I would have no work. But that is not the way of the world. The way of the world is that holes open. Not just in battered old suit jackets that mismatch their pants like some young men I know go about the streets wearing for reasons that elude me. But in marriages and civilizations and tribes and clans. You can wonder, as I often have, why holes open, why is the design of a universe in which things fly apart? But then I remember that the work is to repair the holes, to make whole that which has flown apart. You see what I am saying here? You smile, but I know you understand. You are the newspaper fellow collecting stories. I am only a tailor. But think: aren't all the stories you collect in the newspaper essentially cut from the same cloth? Each one is in one way or another a story of a hole opening or a hole being closed. A criminal, such as, for example, Mayor John Bernard Hynes of Boston, can wipe out my entire neighborhood with the stroke of a pen; you report this in the newspaper as news, but really he opens a hole, do you see? Then many people strive to heal the hole. And there are many ways to heal holes. Now, some people will say that the *effort* to heal holes is itself good. I do not agree. If I tried to repair a hole in your battered old suit jacket, for example, but did not actually *do* so, what good is that? You would still be jaunting about with a hole the size of a quarter gaping in your seam, embarrassing yourself and everyone you meet, a nice young man with the newspaper but a hole in his jacket, not to mention it does not match the pants. And this is why you are going to leave your poor jacket with me this afternoon, and I will repair the hole, and the universe will be slightly better off. A tailor cannot in one hour repair a hole the size of the entire West End of Boston, but he certainly can vanish a hole the size of a quarter. What kind of a tailor would he be if he could not do that? Just leave it on the counter. I hope your poor mother will not see her son walking back to the newspaper office in nothing but his awful shirt of Egyptian cotton, without even this battered old suit jacket that does not match its pants. It is a good thing your pants do not have holes that I can see, and if they *do* have holes, do me the great favor of not telling me about them this afternoon. A man can only repair so many holes in one day, and just imagine what it is like for me, a professional of long standing, to have to watch you walk away in that awful shirt of Egyptian cotton, for all the world to see? I avert my eyes. Come back before four for your jacket.

Muirin

When I lived in Chicago, fresh out of college, I spent many hundreds of hours by the lake, which is so much bigger than that which we usually mean when we use the word *lake* that it ought properly to be called an inland sea, or even an oceanlet, perhaps; it was so big that it had tides, and there were unbelievably enormous cargo tankers upon the wilderness of its waters, and it had its own weather; often you would see maps and photographs of terrific blizzards in the lake, while the city waited quietly in a thin shiver of wintry light.

First from awe and then from something like reverence, I became a student of the lake and its denizens and cultures, from the shoals of tiny fish who swept along the shore and sometimes died in vast thousands at a time, cramming harbors with silvery redolent drifts, to the taciturn men who crewed the barges and tankers, to the enormous sturgeon that lived in the deepest acres of the lake, to the cheerful and brightly feathered weekend sailors, to the cops who patrolled the shore. And it was one of these police officers who told me a story about the lake one day that I never could forget. I have turned this story over and over in my mind in the many years since I ran along the lake every afternoon with my basketball, spinning around startled ladies walking their tiny dogs, and I still do not quite know what to make of it; perhaps you will know.

The policeman was a burly older man who looked sleepy but wasn't. He had been assigned to my neighborhood for two years, and he patrolled his beat on foot, resorting to his car only on days of unbelievable snow. In his two years he had made a concerted effort to meet and greet every resident—a heroic task in that there were thousands of people in what amounted to a village. But he was not boasting when he said he knew nearly everyone; often I would stand with him for an hour, chatting about this and that, and he would in that time greet fifty people by name, and ask after their children, and pets, and recoveries from various ills and ailments. He had the odd ability, perhaps honed by his profession, to be cheerfully telling me a story with his mouth while his eyes worked elsewhere; one time I remember him telling me a story about a sturgeon when he saw a kid fall over the seawall two blocks away, and he took off running so fast that the sentence he had just spoken trailed after him an instant before it blew away in the wind. There was always a brisk wind cutting in off the lake.

The story he told me that I never forgot, though, was about a woman who lost her son when he was five months old. The woman lived near the venerable old Majestic Hotel, right by the lakefront, and the policeman saw her walking every day, and he told me the whole neighborhood was thrilled when she had her baby, and the whole neighborhood was plunged into gloom when the baby died in his crib. After he died she didn't emerge for a while, and then when she did emerge and walk along the lake again, she was silent and dark, and no one could cut through to who she used to be, not even the policeman, or the gentle old Navy veteran Mister Pawlowsky who knew everyone, or Mister Pawlowsky's wise and entertaining dog Edward, who roamed freely in the neighborhood and was much liked and respected by all, even cats.

One summer morning, though, as this woman was walking along the lake, she saw something struggling in the shallows, and she ran down to the beach, and found a baby wriggling and thrashing at the edge of the lake. She wrapped it in her jacket and carried it back up to the seawall path, and luckily the policeman was just happening by, at the beginning of his day, so he took her and the baby to the hospital. The baby was healthy, no one could find any trace of parents or identification, and the local alderman interceded to allow the woman to adopt the child. During the process of adoption, the child, a boy, was cared for by the woman, on the single condition that she check in with the policeman every day about problems, forms, insurance, and other matters of that sort. By the time the adoption was officially approved and all forms filed, the boy was a year old, and the neighborhood celebrated his birthday with an impromptu picnic on the beach where he had been found. The policeman, at the woman's request, found a priest to baptize the child, using water from the lake. His mother named the boy Muirin, which means born of the sea in Gaelic, and the policeman told me that the boy, suitably enough, was totally absorbed by the lake, and was already a fine fisherman, young as he was.

I see that kid every other day, I bet, said the policeman, and you will too, if you keep your eyes peeled. Next time I see him I will point him out. Soon after that conversation, however, I moved to Boston, and never did see Muirin, but I never forgot the story of the boy who came out of the lake to a woman with a hole in her heart exactly his size.

The Seventh

A friend of mine told me a story recently that I cannot get out of my head and it goes like this. A friend of his who everyone thought was happily married slid into an affair with another woman. It's not worth explaining how it happened, said my friend, because it's the usual stupid stuff, he just slouched into it because it was interesting, it wasn't like he was in love with the woman or anything, he actually really loved his wife, it was just that this side trip was interesting and made him feel cool and then he tripped over the line and felt awful. I mean, he was really hammered by what he had done. To give the dude some credit he immediately went to his wife and confessed, and apologized from the bottom of his heart, and was as totally straight and honest about what had happened as you could possibly be, he told her anything and everything she wanted to know, although she's a very cool being and didn't want to know details, she just wanted to know where they stood so she could make her own decisions as to the future and etc.

Then he went to his pastor and confessed to him too, and they had a long talk about the seventh commandment, and he was totally straight and honest with the priest too, which a lot of people aren't, you know, despite saying they are. Any priest will tell you that. Then my friend talked to his friends, explaining why things were awkward with him and his wife, and they were declining dinner invites and invites to games and things like that, and he and his wife went to counseling, and to marriage encounter, and had weekly meetings with the pastor about reconciliation and forgiveness, and to be honest his friends, including me, thought that they actually might work things out, mostly because his wife is a very cool being and if anyone could ever find a way past being betrayed by your spouse, she could.

But then something snapped, and that's the nut of this story. He told me he didn't feel like he was shriven of his sin, and he was uncomfortable all the time, so one day he goes to the golf course to play nine, just to relax, you know, to get out of his head for a while. He plays through six at one over par—he's a real good golfer—but he gets stuck at seven. Seven is a par four, probably 300 yards, but it's a dogleg, with huge trees at the turn so you can't just hit over them, and there's an evil bunker right before the green, and a little thirsty creek right past the green. Hell of a hole. I've never played it in less than six, and I am a decent golfer. Anyway, my friend shoots a seven on the seventh, and something snaps in his head, and he goes right back to the tee box to play the hole again.

Now, this is bad form to begin with—you are supposed to just play through whether or not there are other guys on the course, that's the way you play the game—and it's particularly bad form when there's someone behind you, which there was. My friend has a chat with the guys behind him, though, and he's a good guy, everybody knows and likes him, so they let him play the hole again ahead of them, and he shoots a seven again, and comes right back to the tee box. This time the guys play the seventh themselves, staring back at my friend, and he waits patiently until they hole out and then he plays the seventh for a third time. This time he shoots an eight. He goes right back to the tee box and plays the hole again. Six. He goes right back to the box and this time the course manager comes out in his cart and says what the hey? My friend says he has to shoot par on the seventh come hell or high water. The manager understandably basically keeps saying what the hey for a while and then he figures it's a slow day, play it all day if you want, but every nine times you play the seventh you owe me the cost of a full eighteen, which is a fair fee for nine holes plus a nine-hole penalty for weirdness. My friend says fine and that's what he does, he plays the seventh the rest of the day, like ten more times, and he shoots a five twice, but he just cannot get down to par, this hole is a killer, and it doesn't get easier when you're tired or angry. Those trees are huge, with serious branches, and that creek has guzzled thousands of balls over the years, and that's a nasty little bunker with those sharp vertical walls like a tomb or something. Why they make bunkers like that is a mystery to me. It's just cruel. It doesn't reflect any kind of natural hazard on the course.

Finally the light fails and my friend can't play anymore but something's snapped in his head, and he goes home and gets a tent and a sleeping bag and he comes back and camps out by the tee box of the seventh so he's ready to start at dawn. At dawn he's out there ready to tee off in the mist when the manager comes out again in his cart and says what the hey but this time he is not in an amiable mood. My buddy explains that something's snapped and he is going to shoot par on this hole or else. The manager thinks about calling the cops but he knows my buddy and he knows what happened as regards the seventh commandment and he figures the whole point of being neighbors in a town is to cut each other a little slack when something snaps, so he reroutes play for the day, putting up Course Under Repair signs, and goes back to the clubhouse thinking interesting thoughts.

Well, my buddy was there all day. It was a Tuesday. He tried every possible approach to that hole. He tried to hit over the trees. He tried laying up at the turn and then hitting to the flag. He tried laying up right before the trees and hitting an eight as high as he could, like a huge flop shot. He tried shooting right into the bunker and then lashing out with the wedge. He tried hitting into the creek and hitting a wedge back up onto the green. He even tried hitting to the next hole over and approaching the seventh sideways. I mean, he tried every conceivable combination of shots possible on that hole. I think he invented a couple of new approaches. People started to gather and watch. First it was other golfers on the course who saw him working so hard and then it was people in the neighborhood and finally his wife came and watched for a while. Before she showed up he was starting to tire and shoot eights and nines, but once she arrived he shot a six and then a five. She was going to say something to him at that point, I think, but she didn't. She just stood among the trees and watched. He shot another five, *just* missing a long putt for four, and he sat down on the green and put his head in his hands. She walked up to him at that point and said something to him and they walked back up the hill together toward the tee box, not holding hands or anything but walking together, but then they walked right past the tee to her car and she drove him home. Myself and another guy packed up his tent and clubs and stuff for him. I didn't see my friend for a few days after that but the next time I saw him I asked him what his wife said to him on the green and he said it wasn't something he could share but that it was a piercing and hopeful remark, which personally I find refreshing. In that same situation, you know, how many wronged spouses would be able to summon the grace to stroll out of the trees down to the seventh green and make a piercing and hopeful remark? Maybe more than we know.

Biographical Note

Brian Doyle is the editor of *Portland Magazine* at the University of Portland, in Oregon. He is the author of many books of essays, "proems," and fiction, among them *Bin Laden's Bald Spot* (Red Hen Press, 2011). Among honors for his work are the Award in Literature from the American Academy of Arts & Letters, the Pacific Northwest Booksellers Association Award, and a 2016 Oregon Book Award.

CPSIA information can be obtained at www.ICGtesting.com
Printed in the USA
BVOW02s0853030916

460929BV00002B/9/P